the Unblessed Hand

John Boulton

UK Book Publishing.com

Design, typesetting and publishing by UK Book Publishing

www.ukbookpublishing.com

ISBN: 978-1-918077-17-9

Dedication

---

*To my family and friends
in particular Fate a friend
that has never let my down.*

Table of Contents

Regional Map

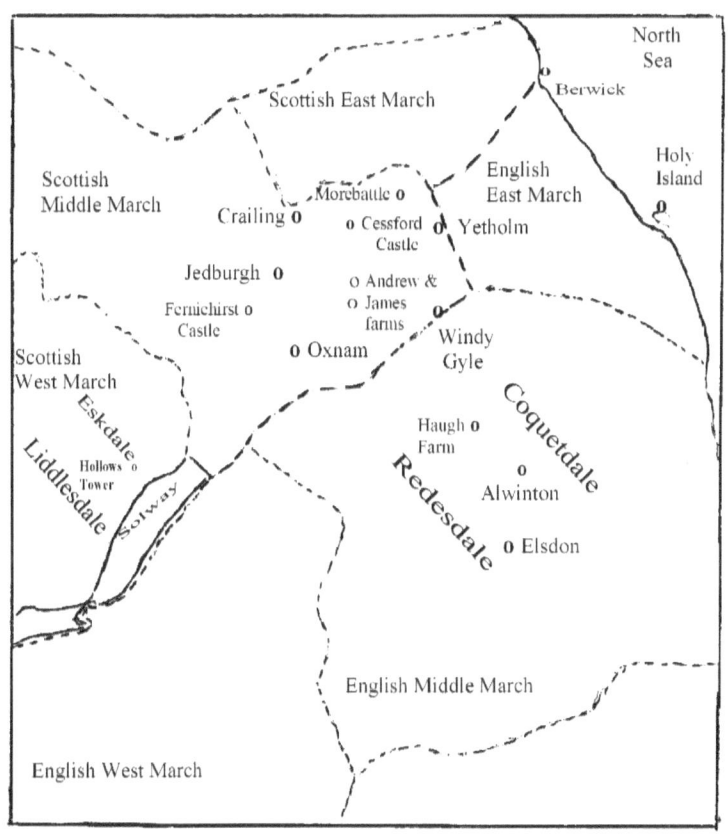

North Sea

Scottish East March

Berwick

Scottish Middle March

Holy Island

Crailing o

Morebattle o

English East March

o Cessford Castle

o Yetholm

Jedburgh o

o Andrew & o James farms

Fernichirst o Castle

Windy Gyle

Scottish West March

o Oxnam

Eskdale

Coquetdale

Haugh o Farm

Liddlesdale

Hollows o Tower

Redesdale

o Alwinton

Solway

o Elsdon

English Middle March

English West March

Foreword

—

I must admit I never liked history at school. Being the eldest of the five children of a coal miner living in the colliery rows of Ashington I could not be further away from royalty. In those days history was mainly about Kings and Queens which was a shame considering the wealth of history we have in this area.

My interest started by accident following lunch at a local pub. I think local pubs are the catalyst for many ventures. I simply said I wouldn't mind walking the roman wall (Hadrian's). My friend got out his diary and said he was free in April the following year. This was almost forty years ago before the creation of the official walk. As I was not very fit I started walking in the Cheviot hills in preparation for the walk.

It was during this training a came across the numerous hill forts many with nearby cup and ring rock carvings. I could not find a lot of information about these so I moved onto the Border Reivers. I read quite a lot about that era and although I would not class myself as an expert I was able to give talks for local rotary clubs.

I found this era very interesting which has prompted me to write this story. It may be useful for me outline the historical background of that time.

The Border Reivers story starts as far back as 1248 when six Scottish Knights and six English Knights met and agreed laws to govern both sides of the border. Three Marches were created on each side of the border that is the West, Middle and East March (see regional map). A Lord would be appointed as warden of each March. In Scotland the warden would be selected from the local major families but in England a warden from outside the area would be appointed. It is debatable which was the best method.

These wardens were responsible for administering the border law and the arranging of truce days when both sides of the border could meet to settled disputes. These six Marches with their own laws almost formed a country within two countries. This situation lasted for over 350 years until the joining of the two Kingdoms in 1603.

I hope the above helps when reading this story which is centered around the 1550 to 1560 period. Being my first novel I doubt it will have any literally merit but hopefully it gives an insight into that era.

Chapter One
A New Beginning

—

O h how I hate the winter they say the Devil does his best work then, hiding in the shadows planning his evil. Thankfully I don't believe in him, although many a dark shadow has been cast over my life its black veil has always been brushed aside by the hand of fate. For my turbulent life I blame neither the Devil nor God but I am a great believer in fate. It was fate I think that has brought me back to where my story began, that is the place of my birth. The winter is over now but my memories of those cold days and nights still linger. As my father was a widower there were only two of us living there. This meant there was very little conversation particularly in the winter as we spend virtually all our time together so there were no new experiences to recount. Conversation concentrated of farm-work but at that time of year were brief.

My duties were to keep the fire alight. This involved chopping logs stored in the barn and keeping adequate stocks in the house. On cold nights my farther and I would sit close to the fire with heavy coats over our shoulders. No matter how large the fire it would only heat your side facing it. It was at these times I wished my father was a merchant in some town or city where going to work was walking downstairs to the shop below.

A servant would keep the fire lit and life would be comfortable. This idea was however a fantasy as I had never been to a city and had not experienced the stench and the putrid air outside. I now know better.

We were visiting my cousin Ella at the farm where I was born and had spent my childhood. Legally the farm belongs to me, it and the adjoining farm which used to belong to my uncle, that's Ella's father, I inherited when my father and uncle John were both killed. As the only surviving male both farms passed to me, this excluded John's wife Esther and her daughter Ella. I felt this was wrong so when Ella married her father's farm was my wedding present to her. She now lives in my what was my father's farm and operates both from there. This is not a problem as originally it was only one farm being split into two between my father and his brother when my grandfather died. I am minded to give Ella my farm as well but at the moment it suits me to have property in both England and Scotland.

The building has changed a lot since my youth. Ella and her husband have kept it in good repair and on occasions I have funded some of the work on the pretence I was protecting my investment. I liked Ella she was strong willed, a bit like me, and she is all that is left of my original family so I do not mind helping out.

The farmhouse originally had just two rooms one a combined kitchen and living area and another being a bedroom. My father had split the bedroom into separate rooms when my mother was expecting me. Her name was Eleanor, my father called her Nell but rarely speaks about her. I think losing her in childbirth is still painful. Ella who is planning a family has added another two bedrooms attached to the other side of the building. As yet these rooms are not required so my wife and I have the use of one and William the other.

Casting my mind back I recall that life here at the farm had been happy enough but sometimes lonely. There were no children to play with and my cousin Ella was still a child. I did have a sheepdog called Mick which was given to me. He was too old to be a working dog but was a great pet. Due to his age I did not have him very long probably only two or three years but we did have fun. Had I not taken him I hate to think what his fate would have been.

We must have covered most of Coquetdale together sometimes being away for hours. Mick would decide when it was time to return to the farm by refusing to go in any direction other than back to the farm. Unknown to me at the time these escapades gave me great knowledge of the river and the Coquet valley which would prove valuable in the future.

My only friend if I can call him that was the local Vicar the Reverend Hall. Ironic really for a nonbeliever like me but he was my friend and still is today. Neither my father or I went to church on a Sunday as my father blamed God for not saving his wife when she gave birth to me. Reverend Hall visited our farm almost every week but eventually gave up on trying bring my father back into the fold. His conversation moved away from the church and he became just a friend visiting from time to time.

I have vivid memories of the times spent with the Reverend Hall. He had not taken to the church as a vocation but more out of necessity. The Halls were gentry from Redesdale so he was fortunate in being well educated. He could read a talent that not all priests at the time possessed. In fact, one local priest confessed that he had never read the bible but had learned enough by heart to carry out his duties. Reverend Hall because of his crippled leg could not work the land or be of much use in lifting or protecting cattle so his family had sponsored his position.

He was an impressive looking man, tall with pitch black curly hair and dark reflective eyes. If not for the church, I am sure he would have enjoyed the company of women. Instead he would spend his evenings in the ale house at Alwinton only abstaining on Sundays. This was strange as when the Popes influence finally diminished with the crowing of Queen Elizabeth marriage was possible. The church objected to priests attending ale houses but Reverent Hall hung onto the old ways. No one seemed to care and it never became an issue, but anyone wishing the last rights was better requesting it during the day or early evening. Invariably it would be in the early hours and often was incomprehensible dribble. As it was given in Latin with great panache they were usually none the wiser and died contented.

He seemed happy enough in that role and enjoyed teaching me extracts of the bible and eventually how to read. My time with him was well spent as I could read fairly well but my writing was poor which I put down as lack of practice.

Today I am heading to Windy Gyle were I spent many a long hour with Reverend Hall. It was a good vantage point and in past years of trouble a guard would have been posted to give advance warning of raids. Everyone was expected to take their part as a lookout even the clergy were not excluded. I remembered sitting there with Reverend Hall on numerous occasions keeping watch. Due to a childhood accident he had a pronounced limp but it did not exclude him from taking his turn, so long as he took a "runner" with him. He always took me as despite being young I was fast and could carry any warning of impending problems.

I never had any occasion to "sound the alarm" so I spent most of the time enjoying the remoteness of the site.

Reverend Hall utilised his time more fruitfully selecting sections of the bible for use in his next sermon.

He was well read and knew not only religion but the whole history of the area. He would point at the hills.

"See that ditch surrounding the top of the hill, that's where the old people lived when the Romans arrived. They had lived there for so long nobody is sure how old these ruins are" He explained

"They lived on almost all the hill tops in what we call hill forts, you can tell as all their ruins are in a circle whereas the Romans always built in squares"

"Why square" I queried

"It was just their way but I know why they built so many, they were scared of us. They even built the great wall to keep us out, and every time they travelled up here they would dig a ditch and fence off their encampment even if only staying for one night. There are lots of square ditches in this area"

He went on.

"The Normans were just as scared. Two years after William conquered the south we massacred a large force he sent to take charge of Northumbria. This brought terrible reprisals. When he wrote his great book listing all his lands and possessions Northumberland was never included. They tell us that all the great castles that we have, and we have more than anywhere else, are in case the Scots attack but we know it is so they can rule in safety hiding behind their great walls.

Yes, we are a warrior race and everyone is wary of the border families"

Once he started talking I would get a full history lesson, but he was always interesting and spoke with passion about the region. I hope eventually to be able to pass on such knowledge to my son.

Today I will take the opportunity to show my son a route that I had previously taken many times before.

My son although only twelve years old was tall and strong with a mop of long blond hair that on this exposed hill blew behind him. The sun highlighted the traces of ginger that he must have inherited from his mother. Everyone said he was the image of me but today for the first time I could see myself in him as he leapt from rock to rock exactly as I used to do. We had called him William, that's William Charlton, the same as my father and I, but I always got Bill which avoided any confusion.

I have a great relationship with my son. He has the advantage of having a mother as well, something I did not have. We often go hunting deer together on my farm in Scotland which incorporates quite a large area of woodland. He is a much better shot with a musket than I am but my strength was always with a sword. Unlike many youngsters he is a great help with the farm and rarely complains no matter the nature of whatever tasks I give him.

It is only now I realise how similar I am to my father. We were both tall and strong but in actions very reserved. Looking at him I feel what I am sure my father felt as well but had difficultly showing it. I try my best to maintain the strong bond we have.

Enough of this pondering I need to concentrate and continue heading forward. The route gave us beautiful views across the hills and valleys and I stopped frequently to enjoy the scenery. Well, this was partly true as I needed regular stops to catch my breath and this gave me the opportunity to hide from William how difficult I was finding the climb. Thankfully half way up the hill there was a long wide flat area part of the drovers' route leading into Scotland. From it you could see the valleys to the left and right, both had streams that appeared as streaks of silver cascading from the hills eventually meandering along the valley floor. I took the opportunity to pause and admire the view while taking a drink of water from the bottle I had carried.

At this point there was a break in the clouds and a beam of light lit up the cairn on top of the hill. I thought is the light showing me the way again as the old lady had predicted. I took another gulp of water and suitably refreshed I pushed on to the final climb. At last we reached the top and found a seat on a pile of stones. The cairn marked the border between England and Scotland.

I cleared a space next to me the beckoned to William

"Here son have a seat and let's enjoy the view"

I did this not purely for pleasure but it also gave me the opportunity to have a rest.

For some reason the cairn was growing as it had become a tradition to add a rock to the pile every time someone reached the top. This we also did as if some stone god would strike us down for being disrespectful if we didn't.

In amongst the rocks I noticed one or two large round pebbles of a different colour from the rest.

"Look at these William someone must have carried them up from the river below"

I thought they must be mad as it was a tough enough climb without weighing one down with heavy rocks.

Another rock was carved with rings. It had obviously been part of a larger one as its rough edges showed where it had been broken off. This to me was more surprising than the coloured ones. These carvings are by the old people and any such rocks are considered sacred and are not usually moved by any locals. Even farmers plough around them rather than risk relocating them.

Enough of this pondering I thought to myself so I stood up and firstly raising my hand to shelter my eyes from the sun I gazed south before scanning to my right then looking directly north.

It was a beautiful day; the sky was blue with only wisps of clouds so you could see for miles.

"All this before us is Scotland"

I said pointing to the north. I could see he was puzzled.

"But it's fairly flat"

He was right except for a few hills in front of us the whole area formed a large cultivated plain. Looking south the massive hills of the Cheviots stretched as far as the eye could see giving the wrong impression that England must be all hills.

Memories of the days spent here with Reverent Hall sitting on the same flat rock that my son and I were now utilising came flooding back. I would lie back and get pleasure from the comforting sound of birds and sheep. Occasionally we would hear the barking of a dog, probably a shepherd rounding up sheep in the next valley. The sheep were the noisiest and would usually start with individual sheep taking turns but sometimes for no apparent reason they would all break out into a chorus that could last as long as an hour.

I liked the autumn best. The hills were a patchwork of different greens and purple which constantly changed as the wind moved the clouds overhead breaking up the sunlight. It was an idyllic spot if not for the wind but there was always the wind.

At this time of year, I often observed a vixen, she would carry a cub and then seem to desert it only to return later with yet another cub. This process would be repeated until sometimes there would be five or six cubs. She would then move them one by one to yet another spot. I could not understand what she was doing but noticed the number of cubs would diminish with time.

I returned to the large flat stone protruding from the cairn, which had become our convenient seat, and as I surveyed the familiar hills my recollections of the past came flooding back together with the strong emotions I still felt from all those years ago. The lazy days I had spent there were as vivid as if only yesterday and it seemed I need only to stretch out my hand and I could grab hold of my memories and pull them into the present. Unfortunately, they were like the wisps of mist still hanging in the valleys, there to be appreciated but would only slip through your fingers if you try to capture them.

Today however, we were just there for the view and to eat the beef sandwiches my wife had prepared. It must have been obvious to William that my mind had strayed as I had been quiet for quite a while. This probably prompted his question.

"Have you been here before?"

He asked in a way that anticipated more than a simple yes or no.

"I have many times"

Was my reply but was loathe to mention one fateful time I had passed this way. However, he pressed for more

"Did you come here with your father?"

I had when I was only a few years older than my son but this was the start of a long story that I had so far withheld from him. I thought the telling could not be as traumatic as having to live it so maybe it was time he knew.

At this point the sun broke through the clouds again as if fate was giving me permission to tell my story.

"Well son" I started "I was a couple of years older than you when I passed this way with my first father"

"Your first father?" was his puzzled response

"Yes" I continued

"You only have me, but in my life I have looked at three men as my father"

Two of them were before my son was born so the grandfather he knew now he had assumed was the only one.

The one I was now recalling was my real father. He had decided that I was old enough to assist in the lifting of cattle and I was proud to be accompanying him. It had been a last minute decision due to the sudden illness of one of the men who had planned go. It had not been intended for it to be a major raid but only to cross the border by a few miles and steal a small number of cows. This quick short raid was not considered to be very risky so there seemed no problem in me tagging along.

We passed the very hill we were sitting on. It is called Windy Gyle and is adjacent to a droving route which was the way we meant to return with the acquired cattle.

Our party was seven strong that is six men and me. I think I had only been asked as my father thought seven was a lucky number. In charge were my father and his brother John. You could tell they were brothers both had fair hair, blue eyes and the same ruddy complexion. My father was a little taller with a much heavier frame. John was a joker and was always laughing but my father was much more serious maybe as a result of the lack of adult company. My mother had died giving birth to me so he was unable to have the kind of banter John had with his wife Esther. I could not say he wasn't a good father he certainly was but he was never affectionate, the pat on the back or occasional hand on the shoulder were very rare. I never knew what it was like to have a mother so I cannot say I missed her but I did on occasions wonder what she would have been like.

The remainder of our party was four young men who frequented the inn at Alwinton. As I was too young to visit the inn I did not know any of them but had been told they enjoyed drinking and gambling and this was a way of funding their excesses. Although I was introduced to them I can only remember one of their names which was Bob as he was continuously teased by the others. They were all in their mid-twenties but still laughed and carried on like teenagers. The whole escapade to them appeared to be a bit of fun with potential rewards.

It wasn't a moonless night, but pitch black when covered with clouds. Uncle John who was navigating seemed to know every rock, stream and ditch. He kept checking our position using the stars for guidance. I wondered how he had managed to obtain such expertise.

After about two hours we passed through a wooded area which was the north boundary of a field with the other three sides formed by a bend in the river. This enclosed area housed ten cows which would be easy pickings as we numbered almost as many as the cows. My uncle John Charlton said he would take the lead cow if the rest of us followed the river's edge behind the cattle to push them forward. It was a good plan and we were soon well placed to carry it out.

The silence was broken by a crackling sound as if someone had thrown a wet log onto a hot fire only much louder. Two men fell from their horses holding their chests and screaming in pain having been hit by musket balls. One was Bob who had been hit in the chest and almost simultaneously in the centre of his forehead. He fell to the ground directly in front of me with his mouth and eyes wide open staring up at the stars. It was the most horrible sight I had ever seen. Before I had time to think five or six men who had been hiding behind the river bank were upon us. I leapt from my horse and dived behind a fallen tree trunk although hidden from sight I could still hear the shouting and clashing of swords.

I managed to peek between the branches but still concealed. It was an uneven fight as after the musket volley only four men were standing, three of whom were quickly surrounded with no chance of escape. My father fought ferociously against his attacker but the other two were unfortunate in having to tackle two each. It was a slaughter. As they tried to parry the blows from one the other mercilessly attacked their sword arms from behind. Totally defenceless they were attacked from both sides and fell in agony. They were finished off with swords being plunged into their chests

My uncle who was at the other side of the cattle should have taken flight seeing the situation was hopeless yet he still attempted to force his way towards the fight. He was stopped in his tracks by a streak of white which hit him squarely in the chest. It was an arrow. No one uses arrows now I thought but sure enough that's what it was.

I had watched the men of my family fall one by one. My father was last. I was astonished how good a swordsman he was and still don't know how he acquired such skill. He had killed one, and then mortally wounded another when he went to assist his friends, but was eventually overwhelmed by force of numbers. He had forced back one attacker only to be struck from behind by another virtually severing his right arm. He fell to the ground and tried to retrieve his sword with his other hand but before he could reach it a huge man stood over him. He delivered the fatal blows in frenzied attack like a madman out of control. The sound of his sword crashing down and my father's groans as he took his last breath still haunt me today.

I took careful notice of this man as I meant to kill him. He was a tall man with a slight limp probably from an old wound. His long hair hung loose on his shoulders covering his features but unable to hide a scar which ran almost the full length of his face. He was a frightening sight and had the look of a man not to be trifled with.

However, being only a boy on his first raid no one considered it necessary to provide me with any weapons. But lying beside me was a broken branch about the size of a man's arm. I picked it up and ran at him only to be confronted by one of his men. I swung at him with all my might but he was quick and side stepped me. I caught his belt with the ragged end of the branch, it snagged and he swung me round like a dog on a lead. There were screams of laughter as his companions watched this spectacle.

"You've never caught one that big before" someone shouted.

The humour of the moment escaped me as he slammed me against a tree and I fell to the ground gasping for air.

I looked up to see a boy standing over me. He was young but a few years older than me. He had a quiver of arrows strung to his back and held a bow in his right hand. He was good looking, not big in stature but looked fit and agile. I then caught a glimpse of the sword above me.

"No father" he shouted lifting his bow.

"He's only a boy"

"Alright Cubby but what else can we do with him?" his father asked.

It was then the man whom I was sworn to kill stepped forward, he was obviously the leader.

"You keep him you seemed to be attached to him"

He uttered to great hilarity.

I was led away into the darkness knowing that a chapter in my life had just ended and wondering if it would be the last.

We followed the river further north. No one bothered to tie me up to prevent me escaping. I thought of diving into the river, but as it was early spring the water from the hills not only flowed fast but was icy cold. Anyone falling in would not survive the night without the aid of a good fire. Even so where would I go, my father was dead, my mother had died giving birth to me and I had just witnessed the death of my nearest kin. I was in need of food and shelter and hoped for this before the night was out.

As we rode riders peeled off heading for their various farms. My father's killer and a wounded man were the last to leave us.

"See you in a couple of days James and thanks for your help"

"Any time Andrew that's what family is for, I hope the lad will be alright"

This left me with Cubby and his father. When we reached their house I was ordered into the barn with

"There is plenty of straw to make you comfortable and I will get my wife to find you some food".

I made my way inside, sat down on a bale and cried. It was now registering what had taken place. I put my hand in my pocket and took out the medallion I had been given on my tenth birthday. It was not valuable at all in fact it was an old horse brass with the Charlton coat of arms. My father had the local blacksmith modify it and as he could not read Reverend Hall had shown him how to stamp on my name. So long as I have this I would remember my father.

The door opened and in came Cubby's mother holding a candle and a bowl of lamb broth. She was not a tall woman, stocky yet not fat. She had bright rosy cheeks and a healthy glow; in fact, she looked the typical farmer's wife.

"Here you are son you must be cold".

She looked at me kindly then took the corner of her apron and wiped the blood from my brow where I had had the encounter with the tree. I had never known my mother so her compassion born out of maternal instincts was foreign to me. I looked up in silence with the tears running down my cheeks.

"Don't worry you will be alright here"

She reassured me. This single act of kindness created a bond stronger than any rope and I no longer thought of escaping.

The next morning, I was fed and put to work stacking fire wood. After a couple of hours, I had finished my task and sat down to catch my breath. That was when Cubby joined me and we talked for the rest of the morning. He told me he was a Cessford part of the Kerr family. He had been christened Cuthbert after the local saint giving him the nickname Cubby. The Kerrs were one of the most feared border families. We had certainly picked the wrong cows to steal. The man who had killed my father was Andrew Kerr a cousin of Sir Walter Kerr the chief of the family. I thought to myself someday I must kill this man but did not utter a word.

"How did you know we were coming?" I asked.

"My cousin was in the ale house yesterday and overheard a conversation"

Apparently my uncle John had told someone not to have too much to drink as they would be riding that night. Riding was another term for reiving. They had a good idea of the route we might take and had driven ten cows as bait to a spot where we could not miss them. Cubby had been the lookout on the adjacent hill. Unfortunately for us there had been a break in the clouds giving enough light for him to see us coming so he was able to rush down to give warning. This gave enough time for their men to position themselves behind the river banks. The ambush was well planned and once we had entered the field we had little chance of escape.

"Why do you use a bow?" I asked.

"I just like it" he replied and went on to explain he could fire five or six arrows before anyone could reload a musket. And if he fired from cover it did not give away his position as there was no flash or smoke and it was virtually silent.

He went on.

"Anyway the bow is much more common than you think. Most people still prefer it to the musket which can be unreliable and sometimes can injure the user"

"You must have done it a lot?" I prompted

"Only for hunting, last night was the first time I fired at a man".

He had killed my uncle but saved my life so I bore him no malice; in fact, I liked him from the start.

Cubby's father was James Kerr of the Cessford branch of the Kerr family. He was a rough looking man who with his wife Ethel farmed a large area bordered by a river to the south and rolling hills to the north. The breeding of cattle was his main business but some acres were left fallow to provide hay for winter feeding and a few growing wheat sufficient for family use. He had a reputation as the best breeder in the area and commanded a good price for his cattle. He was not rich, but comfortable and certainly better off than many of the subsistence farmers I knew south of the border. He only had the one son so had to hire help at harvest time and for hay making. Between the two of them they could manage cattle which were less labour intensive but they had been unable to keep up with general farm repairs. Farm buildings and in particular the miles of dry stone walling had fallen into disrepair. I therefore, was a resource that could be utilised. At least that was what I hoped.

I was left alone in the barn for quite a while which gave me time to survey my surroundings. The barn was large and from the smell had obviously housed some cattle over the winter. There was a ladder leading up to a partially planked area filled with bales of straw. At the end of the barn was a triangular window or more accurately an opening with a planked gate. Obviously used to throw bales through.

Eventually that evening Cubby's father came into the barn and sat on a bale of straw. He looked at me but was silent for so long I wondered if he would speak at all. He had obviously been pondering what to do with me. He got up walked back and forwards for a while with his hands in his pockets and kicked a bale. He stopped turned and looked me. Holding out his hands he spoke.

"I don't know what to do with you. I don't even know your name"

I replied

"It's William Charlton but I usually get Bill"

I could tell he had made a decision.

"Look here Bill, I have need of some help around the farm and if this suits you we can provide for you here. But if you wish to make your way back to where you came from I will not prevent you. The decision is yours so sleep on it and let me know in the morning"

I knew it was an important decision but it was not a difficult one to make. Here there was Cubby who I had already a brotherly affection for and his mother Ethel who had shown nothing but kindness. At home I had never had a brother or mother and with the death of my father and uncle had no close family and an uncertain future. I felt I had found a family here and in the years that followed was proven to be right.

The next morning as I was sitting on a bale eating breakfast that Cubby's mother had brought me he returned.

"Well then what is it to be?"

"I'll stay here" was my prompt reply.

"In that case we will put you to work. Each morning you will chop and stack the firewood for that day and afterwards I will direct you to a section of wall for you repair or rebuild"

I nodded my acceptance.

"Today when you have finished the firewood you can start on the wall adjoining the barn so I can see how you manage"

Luckily for me I had watched my father on a number of occasions and new fairly well how to do this. I passed the inspection that evening and as James left me he patted me on the back

"Well done that deserves supper"

He said smiling as he walked away. After that day I felt part of the family even though I was living in the barn, this did not seem to matter.

In the months that followed as my repair work continued it pushed me further and further away from the farm. Ethel would wrap up some meat and bread as she did for Cubby and James. Often when sitting eating my snack I pondered over what would have happened if I had decided to head for home. Would they really have let me go, the first few weeks I worked close at hand and without a horse would easily be caught? Would the Kerrs want me to report what had taken place? I concluded that it was more likely that I would have an "accident" so I had made the right choice even if for other reasons rather than fear.

Sometimes I would be working where Cubby was attending cattle and he would sneak away and join me. We would eat our food and tell jokes. I was surprised that our laughter did not give us away. I'm sure it did but James did not mind so long as the work was not neglected.

I was happy but still had not forgotten Andrew Kerr. Every time I was on wall duty I would lift the larger stones above my head several times before placing them in position. Each morning I would select a branch and use it to practice swordplay. It did not improve my skill much but over time the branch got heavier and heavier and my right arm stronger and stronger. When I was baptised as was the tradition at the time I was fully immersed in water but held by my right hand so it remained dry. This was so you could deliver unholy blows with the unblessed hand. This I fully intended to do.

As autumn approached the nights were cutting in. One morning as I was chopping wood James arrived leading a pony.

"Here" he said handing me the reigns

"It's getting dark earlier this will let you make the best use of the daylight"

I could not hide my delight.

"You must look after her" was his parting comment. The border ponies where not large but extremely tough and agile. Life was much easier now getting to and from some of the remote parts of the farm used to take a large proportion of the day and unexpectedly with the pony it was not so lonely.

With winter came the snow and this year it was particularly heavy. At night I would bury myself under the straw to keep warm. One night the door opened and in walked Ethel.

"Come with me"

She commanded in a voice which demanded immediate obedience. She took me by hand and led me into the house. Cubby and James were sitting at the table.

"Sit down" she looked at James "You can't leave the boy in the barn in weather like this"

James was definitely the boss but he sensed this was a decision he could not overrule.

"He can share Cubby's room there is enough space for another bed"

I had assumed for some time I was part of the family, but this was confirmation.

Chapter Two
Life at the Farm

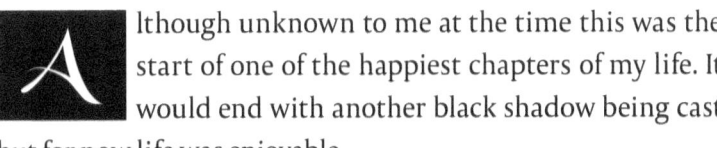

Although unknown to me at the time this was the start of one of the happiest chapters of my life. It would end with another black shadow being cast but for now life was enjoyable.

As the next year progressed Cubby and I became inseparable like two brothers. Or maybe even closer than some brothers as we were best friends as well. We were always joking and were forever looking for our next prank. Then one day a glorious opportunity presented itself.

James had a bull called Samson which was huge and must have weighed the best part of a ton. It was famous as when introduced to the cows never once failed in his duty. One day as we were about to set off for the fields Matthew Kerr from the neighbouring farm arrived. He was to negotiate the use of Samson. Sometimes it was a cash transaction but more usually payment was made with one or more of the offspring. The price was soon settled and it was arranged that in the morning the cows would be brought to the field where Samson was kept. Cubby and I looked at each other smiled and knew this was the opportunity for a prank. That day I worked flat out so I could have some free time to attend the event.

Cubby and I had arranged to meet before the cows arrived. We got there just in time as we could see the cows being led up the valley. As we had planned Cubby arrived with a rope. We tied one end of the rope to a wooden gate post and made a noose at the other end. The idea was to prevent Samson reaching the cows which we thought could be amusing. To get the noose around one of the bull's legs was the problem. Samson was placid and could be approached easily so I crawled up to him and placed the loop of rope on the ground in front of his rear legs. We then lay under the gate and waited for the bull to step into it. This was more difficult than expected as the bull moved either left or right but never stepped forward into the noose. I had to repeatedly replace the noose. It seemed it would never work and we could now hear the cows coming so were running out of time. At the last moment he did and Cubby pulled the rope tight snaring his rear leg. The bull looked up ignored us and continued to graze.

About a dozen cows were led into the top of the field by Matthew Kerr and a couple of helpers. They shut the gate then leaned on it chatting. They did not stay long knowing Samson would perform his duty and that as it was market day their time would be better spent in the ale house. This was a relief to us as otherwise it would spoil our plans.

Samson was at the bottom of the field but had noticed the cows. He was an old hand and would finish his meal before attending to them. Eventually he started to saunter uphill but the rope tightened impeding his progress. He bellowed and charged towards the cows with such strength that he pulled the gate post clean out of the ground. As he ran it hit a large rock protruding from the ground and flew into the air. He was like a child pulling a kite. His charged stopped abruptly at the first cow, which he mounted, but the gate post didn't. With its momentum it shot forward wrapping the rope around the legs of an unfortunate cow pulling it howling into the mud.

Then the performance began with perfect synchronised timing. As the bull thrust forward he was immediately pulled back by the cow trying to disentangle herself from the rope. Thrust and pull, thrust and pull continued for what seemed ages and was so hilarious that we fell upon the ground rolling with laughter until the tears ran down out cheeks. This prank had far exceeded our expectations. Eventually the noose slipped from Samson's leg freeing both him and the unfortunate cow. We had to admire the bull as none of this had prevented him performing his duty. When we recovered we knew we had better hide our tracks as messing with James' pride and joy would not be taken lightly.

"It's a good job we didn't tie him to the post with the gate attached," Cubby laughed.

We retrieved the rope replaced the gate post packing it in with rocks. When James notices it, it will be another job for me. After that day we could not pass Samson without sniggering. We both agreed he had been aptly named. When I look back at this I cannot believe how stupid we were, but I guess that's what boys of that age got up to.

That summer was the happiest of my life. The highlight of each day would be supper when we would all sit round the table and Ethel would serve the meal. She was a good cook and we ate well. Both Ethel and James had a good sense of humour and delighted in leg pulling. One evening Ethel commented

"I'll be serving the Charlton spur tomorrow"

This was directed at me as tradition had it that in my family when meat supplies were getting low the lady of the house would serve up a spur on a salver. This was a hint to the men that it was time they took to their horses.

To Cubby and I this seemed to be a challenge or more likely just an excuse as we needed little encouragement to be mischievous. That night we could easily remedy the problem, or so we thought.

We waited till nightfall and sneaked out. We walked the ponies for a good while so as not to be heard. Our target was Matthew Kerr's farm where we knew he kept pigs. James could not tolerate their smell and refused to have them on his farm so pork was a treat for us. When we got to within quarter of a mile we dismounted walked the horses quietly then tethered them close to the farm leaving us a short walk on foot. Because I had been used to lifting heavy stones it was agreed I should steal the pig. I still couldn't manage a full grown pig so I set my sights on a youngster. I climbed over the wall surrounding the sty and grabbed the pig. The wall was only three-foot-high but with a wriggling squealing pig almost insurmountable. The ground was wet and slimy and I fell into the stinking quagmire still hanging onto the squealing pig; the noise was horrendous and by now must have awakened the whole farm. Cubby leapt the wall to assist but lost his footing on the slippery surface and joined me wriggling in the slime. Together we eventually managed to extract the pig.

By now we could hear shouting from the farmhouse. I held the pig against my hip and ran as if the devil was chasing me. I had got halfway towards my horse when a shot rang out and I felt a dull thud against my thigh.

"I've been shot"

I could feel the blood running down my leg. This made me run even faster, I reached the horse and swung the pig over the saddle and took off. We galloped away into the night. In the panic I had not even noticed the pig was no longer squealing. We reached a point where we felt safe and dismounted to check my wounds. That was when we realised the pig was dead and that it had been shot and not me. We howled with laughter in our relief as we had not until then comprehended the humour of the event.

"Bill you stink," Cubby remarked holding his nose.

"So do you, we had better wash ourselves in the river"

We returned home leaving the pig on the kitchen floor and took to our beds.

Next morning Ethel caught hold of us.

"There's a dead pig in my kitchen is it anything to do with you two"

"Must have crawled there and died" was Cubby's response.

"Been a tough pig" she continued "There are none on this farm so it has crawled a hell of a long way with a musket ball in its side"

"There, it can't be anything to do with us we don't have a musket"

We grabbed our sandwiches and hastened off to work with such speed as to virtually confess our sins. We just about got away with that I thought.

That night as we were about to settle down to supper we had an unexpected visitor, Matthew Kerr.

He wanted to know if we knew anything about a stolen pig and he looked straight at us.

"No, nothing" was our joint response.

"I shot at them" he said "and must have wounded one of them as I heard him shout he had been shot and there was a lot of blood "

"We are all well here "Ethel joined the discussion.

"I can see that, so I'll be on my way"

"Don't rush away Matthew; stop and have a spot of supper were having pork tonight"

She made the offer without even a hint of a smile or conscience.

Oh how I loved that woman. Matthew did not stay as his wife would have a meal ready for him. We enjoyed the pork for supper and all smiled as we ate but not a word of the event was spoken.

After our boyish pranks with the bull and now the pig we seemed to mature and got down to running the farm.

I looked forward to each night when, as a family, we sat together for our evening meal. James had a good sense of humour and could always tell a good tale.

We rarely talked about anything serious but one thing had always puzzled me was why they had named Cubby after an English Saint. So one evening I asked why. Ethel was quick to respond.

"Cuthbert was a monk who travelled the borders long before taking charge of Lindisfarne (Holy Island). He trained at Melrose so he is as much our Saint as yours"

"Yes, maybe" I replied

"But why did you pick that name?"

"It's simple really" Ethel continued.

"James and I never got married in a church but by a travelling priest who preached in the border moving from place to place on a donkey as Cuthbert had done. When I was expecting we were at Melrose market and I took the opportunity to say a prayer in the church. I noticed a dedication to St Cuthbert and decided that if everything went right with the birth that would be the name I would use"

"Good job he wasn't a girl then" I joked

"Yes, but he is pretty enough to be one" James joined in.

"Oh you just cannot be serious for one minute in this house" Ethel rebuked us.

James went on to comment. "We were always going to visit Holy Island but never got round to it. After all it was Scottish monks from Iona that established the Monastery there. Look its quiet on the farm at the moment so why don't you boys take a couple of days off and go there"

"How about it Bill" Cubby seemed keen.

I had remembered Reverend Hall mentioning what to him was a sacred place"

"Why not" I replied knowing there had to be an inn or Ale House on the Island.

Chapter Three
Holy Island of Lindisfarne

—

Next morning the weather was fine so we decided a few days away might be a good idea. We packed our saddle bags with a change of clothes and Ethel produce what seemed to be a week's supply of food. Our visit was taking on the proportions of an expedition.

"Here boys take some extra money and enjoy yourselves" James handed us more than enough money for our trip.

Holy Island was a fair distance but as we had set off early in the morning we would get there by early evening. We took the track up to Morebattle and headed for Berwick then turned south for Holy Island. We were following a route that St Cuthbert had no doubt travelled almost a thousand years before. The border hills are majestic; when the sun shines the shadows form different shades of green. Some hills are quite high so we skirted around them but others we climbed if they were directly in our path.

Eventually we could look down upon the vast coastal plain and see Holy Island in the distance.

It was like a long line drawn on the horizon with two prominent bumps which we assumed were the castle and abbey. A low mist surrounded the Island giving the impression it was floating on clouds. It looked a special place with a mystical feeling.

The tracks lead down a long lane ending at a sandy beach. There we met an old man sitting on a cart obviously waiting for the tide to retreat. We dismounted to rest the horses and walked towards him just to pass the time of day.

"Here boys you may as well have a seat we have a good hour to wait" The cart had a bench seat with plenty of room for the three of us.

"Thanks that's a good idea" I responded climbing up. Cubby grabbed some food which we all shared.

"Are you a local?" I asked.

"Only for seventy years"

He replied with a hint of pride.

Cubby interrupted.

"Excuse our bad manners I should have introduced myself" He apologised

"I'm Cubby and this is my brother Bill"

"Pleased to meet you, I'm John Robson"

"Never, Bill's mother was a Robson it's a small world isn't it" Cubby laughed.

"I thought you said you were brothers" was the puzzled response.

"We're not really but I am an orphan and was taken in by Cubby's family"

"So you are brothers by choice and not by accident of birth, that's got to be a strong bond" The old man was very perceptive.

"Have you any family?" I asked

"I used to have but my wife died some ten years ago. I had a son who left to make his fortune twenty years ago and I have not heard of since"

He paused.

"But I still have a fine life bringing goods back and forward between the Island and Berwick. This keeps

me healthy and provides an adequate income"

"So you must know the tide and the best route across to the Island" I enquired.

"I certainly do, you see that post" He pointed to a post sticking out of the water.

"I put that there and when you can see the bottom of that post the water is no more than a foot deep if you know the way"

"If you know the way" I repeated

"Yes you must keep to the left of that post heading straight towards the Island then follow the coast line to the village"

"Is that the only way?"

"Yes if you don't want to get wet, but we do get some daft monks who take the direct route to the Abbey in bare feet. It is almost a pilgrimage for them"

"Well that's the way for me" Cubby said with confidence.

"This will probably be the only chance I get do this so I am going to do it properly"

"Well I'm following John with the horses" No way was I following Cubby.

John leaned across "You can tie the horses to the cart and sit with me"

We sat watching the water recede. Other than the occasional visit to Berwick this was a rare sight for us. You could see the water moving away, slowly but relentlessly.

John commented.

"You should see the tide come in it is even more impressive; we can go now the whole post is visible"

I checked the horse were secure. Cubby removed his boots and put them in the cart.

"Look after them for me"

"Can I sell them to John when you drown they're a bit little for me?" I teased Cubby

Off he went on a diagonal route heading directly towards the Abbey. John started the cart and moved away at a fairly moderate pace.

"Will he get wet?" I asked John

"Absolutely, the monks usually have someone with them who knows the best way across and even then they often get it wrong"

"Oh what a shame"

I looked at John and we both smiled.

We watched Cubby who seemed to be managing better than I had expected. He was now about half way.

"He needs to go left of those rocks; it's a slight detour but not so deep" John observed.

"How deep is it if he doesn't?" I was concerned.

"He will not drown but it will be chest deep"

I was relieved and watched with interest as he approached the rocks. Will he go left or will he go right I watched with anticipation. Sure enough he went right. He was too far away for us to shout out directions so we had to leave him to his fate. I now felt guilty as I had hoped he would go that way.

Cubby got to within a hundred yards from the end before hitting the deep water. He had gone too far to turn back so he just charged forward. I had to admire him. At times we could see his head and shoulders above water but each time he pushed forward a wave passed over him leaving just his head in view. Eventually he reached the shore to the sound of our cheers and clapping.

"There I knew I could do it but I had better get some dry clothes on I'm freezing"

Cubby managed to say with chattering teeth.

"Jump in the cart I will take you to my cottage and get you dried out" John looked at me

"It's a good job you're not real brothers or you might be as mad as that daft bugger"

His cottage was on the left as you entered the village, it was not large but well kept. The garden was full of flowers of different colours. The door led directly into a room with chairs placed around a log fire which he soon had blazing.

"Thank you for your hospitality John; you have a nice home and a beautiful garden"

"Yes" he replied. "I only do the return trip to Berwick three times a week so it leaves me plenty of time to keep things in order. The garden was my wife's she loved the flowers. It's not practical when I could be growing vegetables, but it makes me feel as if part of her is still here. Silly, eh"

I could feel the medallion my father gave me in my pocket and knew exactly what he meant.

"No it's not silly" I said with conviction.

"Right I'm ready now" Cubby had recovered

"Which way is the nearest inn; Bill is going to buy me a pint as reward for my endeavours"

"It's straight ahead and first right it's only about a hundred paces. They should be able to put you up for the night but if not you're welcome to use my chairs as I only have the one bed"

"Thanks John maybe you can join us later for a drink" I shook his hand firmly.

"I might just do that"

Cubby and I walked to the inn leading the horses by the reigns. We managed to get a room and somewhere to stable the horses and wasted no time in getting to the bar. We could tell it was full of fishermen by the smell. I think they must have just finished gutting fish and needed a drink.

We immediately headed for the bar and ordered our drinks. Cubby asked

"Any chance of ordering some food"

"Of course" The barman replied "would you like"

"What's the choice?" Cubby asked

"Fish or bugger all, what would you like?" was the immediate reply much to the amusement of the locals.

"I think I will have the fish, what about you Bill?"

Cubby joined in with the joke.

So we sat down with our ale and were served beautiful white fish which could well have just been landed by one of the men in the bar.

It was a change for us as the only fish we caught at home were river fish quite different from those landed by boat.

A big rough looking fisherman sitting next to us turned and spoke.

"Down from the farm visiting us are you"

"Aye" was Cubby's short reply.

"It's just a small island so we don't have many farmers here, but lots of fishermen like us so there must be some other reason for visiting"

I thought I had better answer his query.

"My brother is named Cuthbert after your saint and as things were quiet on the farm we thought it might be interesting to visit"

The fisherman laughed. "I'm Cuthbert as well and there is at least another in here tonight, it's a very common name here"

"Come and join us and we will tell you about real men's work, and you can tell us how hard it is lying on the grass looking after sheep"

I then remembered some of Reverend Hall's teaching and retorted with.

"Isn't that exactly what St Cuthbert was doing when he got the call to enter the church?"

"He got you there, the boy's right" One of his pals entered the discussion.

They all laughed aloud. "Buy the boys a pint you mean bugger we have to protect the reputation of us Islanders"

I could not believe this Island we were friends with everyone we had met so far. I thought there must be a reason for this.

We joked and chatted for a couple of hours then in came John carrying a fiddle.

Cuthbert called out.

"Time for some music"

"Does anyone have some pipes?" I enquired.

"The Innkeeper has some can you play them?"

"Not me but my brother can"

John and Cubby played together for at least an hour accompanied by much singing and drinking.

I noticed that most of the fishermen wore similar jumpers. They were dark blue with an elaborate pattern.

I could not help asking Cuthbert about them.

"They're not jumpers I call mine a gansey as does everyone here." Look. He pointed at the shoulder.

"See no seam, they are knitted in one piece by a method handed down from mother to daughter, usually knitted by a mother, wife or sweetheart. "

He pulled at his.

"This was knitted by my wife a couple of years ago. My original one by my mother, when I started fishing, but after years it was well worn out so needed replacing"

"They look very similar" I queried

"They are but every fishing village has their own basic design with slight variation for each individual. You may not know that fishermen are very superstitious and think it is bad luck to learn to swim. No one here can so it makes them extra careful in not putting their boat in jeopardy. But in the event of a disaster if a body is washed up the village it's from can be identified immediately and then the individual."

"Has it happened here" I was curious

"Yes, but thankfully not recently as when a boat goes down it is usually two or three life's lost and often from the same family. Fishing is a dangerous occupation."

"I'm pleased we are farmers the only danger we have is from reivers but they are usually just after cattle and avoid conflict as this can result in a deadly feud."

I was agreeing with Cuthbert but would later wish I kept my mouth shut.

I changed the subject.

"Come on Cubby give us a lively tune and I will get the drinks in."

Eventually our long journey and the drink caught up with us and we decided to call it a night. As we retired our new friend Cuthbert grabbed my arm.

"We're setting our nets at first light if you want to join us be outside the inn when we pass on our way to the boat"

Our beds were clean but uncomfortable so we did not sleep soundly. We awoke early and decided to take up Cuthbert's offer. Luckily we had brought extra clothes so we wore two layers beneath our jackets. Although it was summer Cubby's experience the day before had taught us how cold the water was so we intended to be prepared. We waited in the doorway of the inn sheltered from a strong Westerly wind. Back home the hills gave some protection but here on the Island it gathered the cold from the surrounding sea.

Cuthbert arrived with his two friends who were carrying a large net between them as well as a heavy bucket.

"There I told you they would be here"

He approached

"I'm glad to see you; I've just won a pint from Harry he bet you wouldn't show up"

"Well what else could we do on this small Island?" Cubby said jokingly

"Exactly" Cuthbert replied

We walked past the Abbey which had seen better days. It was in considerable disrepair resulting from neglect since King Henry abolished it among many others. The boat was no more than six or seven paces long but looked sturdy. It had been dragged up onto the beach on a carriage which was basically two wheels at each side of a plank which spanned the centre of the boat. It was an open boat with a canvas canopy at the bow supported by a pole. It was lying with the bow resting in the sand and the stern a couple of feet in the air.

"Right you two put your stuff in the boat and grab the ropes at the front" Cuthbert commanded to his two friends.

"The boys and I will take the stern"

To my surprise the boat was well balanced and it was fairly easy for us to pull down the stern lifting the bows from the sand.

"Now push"

Cuthbert gave such a push it seemed Cubby and I only needed to act as the weight holding the stern down. The boat rolled into the sea floating above its carriage.

"Quick grab that rope"

It was only with Cuthbert's order that I noticed the carriage had dragged a rope behind it. This was sensible, obviously to prevent the wheels floating away. We pulled the wheels out of the water and onto the beach.

"Jump aboard before it floats into deeper water"

We managed to scamper on before the water reached the top of our boots.

"Easy, eh!" Cuthbert exclaimed.

"Usually we have to manage with just three of us"

The other two who we got know were called Harry and George rowed out to sea. It being an Island this did not take too long. We passed between two large cairns one on the south of the Island and another on the mainland which Cuthbert explained were channel markers. To our left on a rocky outcrop the castle towered above us and to our right further down the coast we could see the outline of the massive Bamburgh Castle.

After a good hour rowing Cuthbert decided it was a good place to set the nets. He tossed out a small flag protruding from a large piece of cork. It was attached to the net by a short piece of rope.

"That's so we can find it tomorrow"

The three of us then fed out the net as the other two rowed in a straight line. Another flag was attached to the other end.

"That's the easy bit it's a damn sight harder to pull the bugger back in"

I could see Cuthbert's point and was pleased we would not be back tomorrow to find out.

"Now Harry let's see if we can find the pots"

Cuthbert moved to the front of the boat, placed his hand against his brow to protect his eyes from the sun which was still fairly low in the sky.

"There they are Harry straight ahead"

We stopped next to a small flag and Cuthbert grabbed the rope attached to it.

"Here Cubby you can pull the first one up"

The rope was handed over.

Cubby pulled the soaking wet rope and as he did so the boat tilted and although in no danger of sinking that side was low in the water. It was so low in fact that the wind was blowing water from the tops of the waves into the boat. Eventually the pot popped out of the water causing Cubby to slip and for it to fall on top of him. He screamed as this clawed monster inside tried to grab him through the mesh.

Cuthbert also screamed but in laughter.

"Caught your first lobster or has it caught you"

He held the pot in front of Cubby.

"Here open the hatch and get it out, Bill can put in some fresh bait"

"No bloody way that thing will have my hand off"

Cubby was not stupid.

"I'll show you how to do the first one then you can do the rest"

At this he put his hand into the pot and held the lobster directly behind its nippers.

"If you hold it like this it can't nip you"

He then threw the wriggling creature into a large box.

"Now Bill fetch me that bucket and put in some new bait"

I did exactly as he requested; got the bucket but when I lifted the lid discovered it was full of fish heads and what I assumed were fish guts. It stank like hell.

"Don't be a baby just grab a hand full and toss it in"

I duly obeyed much to Cubby's amusement.

"Cubby throw it back in and pull up the next one"

Cubby coped much better with the second one and managed to get the lobster out and into the box.

After several lobster pots the combination of the spray, wet ropes and wriggling wet lobsters had Cubby thoroughly soaked.

"I've not been on this Island for a whole day yet and this is my second soaking"

Cubby complained but I could tell he was enjoying the experience. I lost count of how many lobster pots there were. There were however enough for me to have to scrape the bottom of the stinking pail with my bare hands to bait the last one.

"I think that's enough for the day it's time for the boys to taste the fruits of their labour. Right Harry lets head for home"

Cuthbert was obviously the man in charge.

"Do you want Bill to give you a spell rowing he hasn't done much else"

Cubby was offering my services.

"No way, it's not as easy as it looks, he would probably have us circling for hours, and I'm hungry"

I was relieved Cuthbert was sensible enough to turn down the offer.

We returned and beached the boat. Cuthbert's wife Hilda was waiting with a hand cart. We loaded our catch onto the cart and I offered to pull it for them.

This time my offer was accepted.

As we passed the Abbey men were loading stones onto carts.

"What's going on here" I asked Cuthbert.

"They're the Queens vandals they're dismantling part of the old Abbey and using the stones to reinforce the castle"

Cuthbert was obviously not happy about it.

"They will not go to heaven, but we will, us fisherman and shepherds get a special mention in the bible"

At this he put his hand on my shoulder.

" That's right isn't it Bill"

"Of course" I agreed

"And if you ever get a chance to visit us Cubby and I will show you how to be a good shepherd"

"Is that difficult?"

"Yes" Cubby butted in

"It takes years of practice lying on the grass on a sunny day watching those noisy animals. Bill and I are still not fully trained but are prepared to stick it out for a few more years"

"You boys should have a walk around the Island it's beautiful this time of year. I will get Hilda to cook some lobsters for you and we will see you in the inn tonight"

Cuthbert shook our hands and we set off to do exactly what he had suggested.

That night we tasted lobster for the first time. It was not fish like and considering the sort of food it ate was surprisingly tasty. We sat drinking with Cuthbert and his two friends. We talked about everything including life on the Island. I enquired why everyone was so relaxed and friendly.

Harry tried to explain. Being an Island everyone knew everyone else. No one was rich and sharing was a way of life. You did not need to steal anything from a neighbour if you wanted it he would lend it to you. None of the houses were fortified and no one bothered to lock their doors.

"What about outsiders" I asked.

Harry continued.

"You can't get on this Island without being noticed you can be spotted from a mile or two away. If on the rare occasion something was for example stolen there is only one way off and they can easily be caught. So even outsiders are not a problem"

"So lifting cattle does not happen?" I queried

"No" Was the reply

"Except for the cow, go on Harry tell him about the cow" George said with a broad smile.

"Aye the cow, it's a good example of what I said. If anyone was to steal cattle there are two problems, one is the cattle don't like the water and need to be forced to cross the other is you would need to know the quickest way across otherwise the tide could catch you"

He paused for a mouthful of ale.

"All we know is that one morning George found a cow standing beside a jacket and boots. It had a rope tied around its neck so obviously someone had tried to lead it away. We can only assume that the animal resisted and the thief got trapped by the tide and must have decided to swim across rather than risk being caught. They were good boots as well weren't they George?"

George lifted a leg to proudly show them off.

"The jacket didn't fit, but I managed to get the price of a pint for it"

I loved their sense of humour; they may be rough hard working men but they were genuine and showed a rare kindness.

"Are you boys off home tomorrow?" Cuthbert asked.

"Yes" Was my short reply

"Then we had better gets some more in. Five more pints please" Cuthbert gestured to the Innkeeper by holding up a hand with all the fingers parted.

"No let us buy them" Cubby insisted.

"Don't worry you will get plenty of chances to do that before the end of the night"

He was right Cubby and I both paid our round as did George, Harry and Cuthbert after us. It had been such a different day and night that we would never forget it.

I cannot remember finding my bed that night but must have as I woke up in it. Cubby and I did not hear our fishermen friends who must have passed the inn at first light. We discovered the boat had gone by the time we walked down to the beach.

I was sad not to be able to say farewell as deep down I knew we would not meet them again. We returned to the inn collected the horses and made our way across the sand. We stopped for a moment when we reached the mainland and looked back towards the Island. Nothing was said but I knew we both felt the same.

For the next couple of years things went smoothly, the farm was now in much better condition due to my hard work and I now spent more time with Cubby attending the cattle.

I was now eighteen and about six feet tall but lean and had not yet reached my full weight. Cubby was in his early twenties not quite as tall as me, now fully grown yet maintaining his boyish looks. We were a good team and usually worked together other than when I was on wall duty. But this day was different someone had pushed over a long section of wall on the outskirts of the farm. Cubby was pressed into helping and while I finished stacking the fire wood he went ahead and I was to follow.

As I neared I could see a number of men heading towards him. One man wearing a red jack approached him as if wishing to converse but instead struck Cubby who fell to the ground. He was then severely kicked as he lay on the ground. My blood boiled and I charged at him with my horse leaping from the saddle. We fell to the ground and rolled around and I managed to punch him drawing blood from his nose. I was then hit from behind by another. Cubby managed to struggle to his feet holding his ribs. I realised we were both in dire trouble so I grabbed him forcing us both into the river. Our attackers were heavily clad and would not follow.

The river flowed away from our farm so we had no chance to return home for help. Our only chance was to head for Matthews farm. Cubby was badly hurt so I had to drag and half carry him. Thankfully Matthew saw us coming and realised something was wrong and galloped up to us. We got Cubby onto the horse and to the farmhouse where he was given a bed. Matthew gave me a horse "You had better get James".

I raced home and collected James and we returned immediately. Cubby was in great pain and obviously had broken some ribs.

"How are you son?"

"Not so bad now, but if it hadn't been for Bill God knows what state I would have been in"

"You should have seen him dad, he charged at them like a knight to the rescue"

"If there hadn't so many I'm sure they would have scattered"

"You had better stay here until you feel better I am sure Matthew will look after you"

James looked at me "Bill would you recognise them"

"Definitely the one that was kicking Cubby"

"That's good enough for me; can I borrow a couple of your men Matthew?"

"Of course but I'm coming as well"

The men put on their jacks these are a leather jacket reinforced by stitching in pieces of steel in the shape of diamonds. They were strong yet flexible and gave reasonable protection. Each took a sword a small pistol called a dag and a steel tipped lance. I was loaned a jacket and sword, the idea was for me to look the part rather than take action, and I was needed for identification.

All five of us looked a formidable force when we headed off. We knew the gang had not headed to our farm or Matthews as we would have passed them. That left only one direction they must be following the river heading west. The river took a long winding route and James calculated that if we rode over the hills we could cut them off.

After two or three hours we clambered down the last hill into the valley. We took shelter in a copse and waited. James was right eventually a group of six men approached.

"Here son take my lance and form a line with the others"

"Which one was it?"

"The one with the red jack"

"When I move forward don't follow but show yourselves so they know you are there"

James headed forward got off his horse and walked towards them.

"This is going to be fun" Matthew whispered into my ear.

"Hey you, yes you with the red jack"

"Picked a fight with my sons have you, how about trying a fully grown man?"

"Yes, you can be brave when you have men armed to the teeth with you" was the reply.

"My men will not take part and neither will yours unless you risk a deadly feud with the Kerrs"

"Fair enough what weapons would you like?"

James smiled "Feet and fists seem to be your favourite so that will do for me"

The man in the red jack dismounted dropped his sword as did James.

"That's a big mistake" Matthew again whispered.

He swung at James with his right hand. He dodged letting it pass his right ear and unleashed a crashing blow into his ribs. He gasped and as he turned felt the full weight of a boot in the groin. As he doubled up with pain a knee crashed into his face. He fell onto his knees only to receive a sound kick in the ribs. I swear I hear the crack of bones. He screamed in agony riving on the ground. At this point his gang moved forward. James drew his dag and pointed it at the nearest.

"It's over" he said "No one needs die today, but let that be a lesson, keep off my land, and touch my sons again and someone will die"

I noticed he said sons twice not son.

Matthew added "Told you, James never lost that sort of fight, it's a good job it wasn't swords he's even better with them"

He climbed back on his horse and I handed him his lance.

"Come on Bill we best hurry home I'm sure Ethel will be worried"

Then he leaned over and whispered in my ear

"I bet Cubby gets pork tonight the lucky bugger"

We laughed out loud at our private joke.

Chapter Four
The Warrior

—

Cubby was still recuperating at Matthew's so James and I were left alone to run the farm together. I must admit that Ethel was as good as any farm hand and easily handled Cubby's mucking out duties. James and I had to work harder than usual but luckily it was not a busy time of year and my wall repair duties were put on hold. I missed Cubby but in some respects it allowed me to work closer with James. This together with the comments James made regarding his sons to Cubby's assailant I now looked at him as my father but without forgetting or being disrespectful to my real father. I still carried the medallion my father had given me but it now evoked mixed emotions I missed him but on the other hand I was now happier than I had ever been. Maybe I just think too much and should accept the hand that fate has dealt me as so far there has been little I could do about it.

James had a small piece of land separated from the main farm by the river. It was an inconvenient location so he rented it to the farmer whose land it was adjacent to. It did not generate much money but gave James an excuse for a monthly visit to the land agent in Jedburgh to collect the rent and spend an evening in one of the many inns. This month he felt it was inconsiderate to leave the farm shorthanded so he asked me to collect the money for him but I was under strict instructions not to spend it all on ale. I could stay overnight and socialise but with moderation.

James gave me a letter of authority but I was to collect the money next morning before returning home. He also gave me sufficient cash for my night in the inn. It was not a case of trust so he said but he did not want to put me at risk by having to hold cash overnight. I was not the least bit offended as I could see the sense in it; anyway I was excited at the opportunity to have a night out. This would be a first without Cubby.

I had finished my duties so was able to mount my horse and head off to Jedburgh. It was a beautiful day with a blue sky broken by white clouds stretching out like wisps of smoke blowing in the wind, there had been recent rain so the air was filled with the fragrance of wet grass. I was alone among the hills soaking up the atmosphere without a care in the world so much so I paid little attention to my direction. I was travelling south and needed to branch off and take the track heading west which was the direct route. I had missed my turn off by a mile or so but was sure the next track leading west would still get me there although by a slight detour. Anyway I had plenty of time and was enjoying the journey.

Unknown to me I had now entered Ferniehirst land. That's when I met her for the first time. She charged up to me with her red hair blazing in the sun.

"Get off my land" she commanded

"This is a public track" I retorted

I was adamant, anyway no girl especially one who was obviously a mere teenager was going to speak to me like that.

"This track leads to our castle and nowhere else so you have no right to be here"She was resolute as well.

"Surely it leads past the castle then on to Jedburgh where I am heading" I was now trying to appear more reasonable.

"Maybe it does but you will have to go back as I am not giving you permission to travel that way" She was not giving an inch.

She was now annoying me.

"You couldn't possibly have the authority to prevent me so I am continuing on my way"

"Here is my authority" She shouted pointing a pistol at my head. "Turn around or I will shoot you"

"No you'll not" I said with confidence as surely no one would shoot an unarmed traveller. I was wrong.

A shot rang out and I felt a sharp pain as it grazed my right ear. The noise spooked her horse which reared up causing her to fall to the ground. I leapt from my horse and pinned her down by grasping her arms and straddling her waist. It was not until then that I realised how beautiful she was. Although still young and with freckles her face was framed by red hair and her bright blue eyes stared at me without a hint of fear.

"I knew you were up to no good, will you take advantage of a woman who is now defenceless"

She was wriggling like a slippery eel.

"I mean you no harm, I had just missed my turn off and was taking what I thought was an alternative route. If I let you up will you behave and let me explain" She nodded so I let her up and we sat together on the grass.

"Good God woman you shot me, I could have been killed. Look I am bleeding. All I wanted was to get to Jedburgh"

I think by now she understood I was genuine. This did not prevent a hint of a smile when she sheepishly uttered.

"Sorry"

"Sorry! Do you not know how embarrassing it would be to be killed by a young girl like you?"

She laughed out loud.

"It would have been dead embarrassing"

I couldn't help but laugh as well.

"Well what are we going to do now?" I asked

"Come on I will lead you to the Jedburgh road"

As we mounted up she commented

"I only meant to fire over your head to give you a fright but my horse moved which affected my aim"

"Stupid horse is to blame then? Anyway a young girl like you should not tackle a man when she is on her own"

I let her know I thought her actions to be foolish.

"It was only you had there been a few of you I would have ridden to the castle for help. We have had a lot of trouble lately and have lost a few sheep so I am wary of strangers"

She tried to explain but I still thought she has been silly.

She led me past Ferniehirst castle and onto the Jedburgh road. I must admit I was very impressed by the castle and wondered what connection she had with it.

As we parted I had to ask

"What's your name I should at least know who shot me?"

"Can't tell you that we haven't been properly introduced"

She smiled, turned away and headed for the castle.

She paused just for a second and turned round laughing

"Don't worry I will soon be out of earshot"

She would be difficult to forget. The rest of my journey was uneventful and I eventually was settled in the inn that James had recommended.

I enjoyed a good steak and a couple of pints of ale. The barmaid was curious about my ear which although only grazed was quite red and swollen.

"Caught on a branch, will look where I'm going in future"

It was the least embarrassing answer I could give which I repeated to James when I returned home the next morning.

It was a few days before Cubby returned. It was then that James got us together.

"I'm sorry boys I did not expect any trouble our farm is fairly remote and things have been peaceful for years"

"In future we must be more prepared so I will teach you how to use a lance and sword. Ethel will stitch you new jackets and I will buy a couple of helmets when I get the chance. We will start tonight when you finish the day's work"

So this began our training. That night James produced two wooden swords. I had never seen them before but apparently they had been used by James's father to teach him. They were rough but about the same shape and size as real swords. I noticed slots had been cut along the length and they had been filled with lead. This gave them the correct weight and balance. I would become very familiar with both ends of them.

"Right Bill I will start with you Cubby is still a bit tender"

I thought we were only fencing and surely Cubby could manage that. I was wrong. We stood facing each other.

"See if you can hit me with your sword"

I swung the sword only for James to parry and at the same time kick me on the thigh. My leg felt dead and as I limped backwards he thumped me on the side.

"I will teach you to fight, not just fence. You're not here to look good but to learn how to win by any means"

He was right, each bump and bruise was a lesson learnt and not easily forgotten.

For the next few months I would go to bed aching but never from hard work. I still practised with a heavy branch when carrying out my firewood duties. As the farm walls were now in good repair I had less opportunity to exercise with the heavy stones so I would utilise any suitable object I could find in the barn. I would be ready for the day I faced Andrew Kerr, my revenge was the only incentive I needed.

I never got the better of James, he was extremely quick and a natural fighter. That was until one day as we were fighting my strength began to tell and I was able to force him backwards. He fell and as he did so I was able to kick his rear end and then again before he was able to regain his composure. He just rolled on the grass laughing heartily. I reached out my hand to help him up. Still laughing as he arose.

"It's a long time since I got my arse kicked" he smiled

"But twice is taking a bloody liberty"

"I'm getting too old for this; I think you and Cubby can practice together in future, there's not much more I can teach you"

That was the end of our training. Cubby and I still practised but not as often, but enough to keep our hand in. We were evenly balanced, Cubby was slightly quicker, like his father, but I was stronger and learnt to anticipate. I could interpret each slight turn or dip of the shoulder and be ready for his next move. This skill would save my life many times in the future.

Over the next few months there were no signs of danger. When rumours were ripe about trouble nearby we would wear our jackets and strap a lance, sword and our helmets to our ponies. We felt safe but in reality it was false security as if there was to be a raid there would probably be several men.

This would be too much for just the two of us no matter how good we were.

We were men now and had the self confidence that came with youth but had now been reinforced by our training. We were afraid of no one. James allowed us to pay frequent visits to the ale house in Morebattle subject to the work requirements of the farm. I remember my first visit there.

The building from the outside looked like a run-down cottage a sign hanging on a pole showed a cockerel standing on a beer keg and was the only indication of the buildings purpose. The roof was thatched but obviously some time ago as it was black with lighter patches where it had been repaired several times. It was in dire need of a full replacement but as long as it was water tight it was good enough for the needs of the customers. Inside was not much better. The walls were bare, the floor flat stone slabs, uneven with large gaps between. The smell of ale was overpowering as any spillage would settle between the stones. One wall was hidden by rows of beer barrels stacked on their sides some with taps hammered in. In front of these was a bench with usually a serving maid between. The landlord would collect the money and only if it got busy would he reluctantly assist in serving. The maids were very friendly and we got to know some of them very well. We had some great nights there. Cubby would borrow the landlord's pipes and a couple of locals played fiddles. There would be music, singing and of course drinking until the early hours.

It was on these nights that we appreciated our mounts. Our "Galloways" were not pretty but clever animals. So long as we could climb on and not fall off they would take us all the way home without any need for our guidance. Sometimes we could not even manage this.

It was on one of these visits I met the Ferniehirst brothers for the first time. They were Kerrs but the Ferniehirst part of the family and were rivals of the Cessfords and sometimes at feud. Currently the relationship fell short of feud but was still not friendly. This animosity was a couple of hundred years old and originated from the rivalry between the two sons of the first Kerr to settle in the area. A Cessford being caught alone by the Ferniehirst family was liable to be beaten up and at other times much worse.

John Ferniehirst looked at Cubby and recognised him as a Cessford.

"It's the son of a bastard father and his whore"

Cubby went quiet.

"Come on Andrew let's get rid of this heap of shit this place stinks badly enough without him".

He had not noticed me or maybe was unaware who I was. As he passed me he went to draw his sword but I held his arm leaving it in its scabbard and struck him with the hilt of my sword knocking him to the ground. I then pointed my sword at John; Cubby was poised ready to tackle his brother.

It was then the landlord stepped between us.

"You Kerrs can carry on fighting outside but not in here."

"You should be more careful who you let in here" Cubby was fuming.

"I am" the landlord replied

"I only let people in who can pay"

He then pointed to John who had picked himself up.

"You and your brother stay across there".

Then, pointing at us.

"Put your swords away and stop in the other side of the room; and in future all of you leave your feuding outside"

That was the end of it and on future rare occasions when we met we just kept out of each other's way.

Things at the farm were quiet. Cubby and I often would finish our chores and go fishing. Ethel never relied on us being successful as we usually weren't. Any trout we caught would be supper the next day. Cubby would quite often disappear for hours as he liked the solitude of riding alone. He would always return refreshed. I thought I might try it sometime but never got round to it as I much preferred to relax by fishing.

We worked hard and I am sure this was appreciated by James. I think this was why he asked us to carry out a chore for him. It was a chance for us to get away from the farm for a day.

"Things are a bit quite here, could you boys pop over the border and check out the price of livestock in Alwinton"

He gave us some money and sent us on our way with.

"You need not rush back"

He knew we would spend it in the ale house and that it would enable me visit the area of my youth.

I had been a boy of fourteen when I left, I was now twenty, six feet tall, muscular and almost a completely different person.

As we descended over the brow of a hill we noticed a couple of people crossing a narrow stream. You could hardly call it a ford as it was no more than two paces wide but nevertheless they were having great difficulty in getting their donkey to cross. As we got closer it was clear that they were an elderly couple. It was then she looked straight at me. Both of her eyes were pure white so she was obviously blind but this stare disturbed me. It was as if she had looked directly into my sole.

I dismounted to give assistance. Reaching out I managed to get hold of the harness and dragged the uncooperative animal to the other side of the water. Then I grabbed the old woman's arm and led her safely over. She was panting for breath and looked exhausted. This incident had clearly been too much for her. I guided her to an outcrop of rocks and sat her down on a flat piece.

"Here have a rest" I suggested

"Thankyou young man, I think I need one"

She was frail and looked as if she needed a good feed.

"Cubby I think it is time for our break, get out the meat and bread Ethel has prepared for us"

I could tell he understood my intentions.

He emptied his saddle bag.

"She has given us far too much again" He then gestured to the couple.

"Come on help us eat this as she always complains if we take any back"

Who we assumed was the husband reluctantly agreed.

"You boys are ever so kind"

We all sat down together. I wondered what an old couple and a heavily laden donkey were up to. I had to enquire.

"That's a lot of stuff you have on that animal"

"Yes I know" He replied

"It's everything we own; we had to move out of the area and are trying to get to Tynedale where my wife has family"

"You had to move?" I continued to question.

"Yes, since my wife turned blind she seems to be able to understand things that ordinary people miss. I had put it down to the fact that her hearing and touch were much keener to compensate for her loss. But I'm not so sure now, she seems to have developed a new sense altogether"

He had now got my interest.

"What do you mean another sense?"

"Well she seems to be able to tell if people are being truthful or have any worries or in some cases what lies in store for them"

That's a useful ability I thought so I replied.

"There's nothing wrong with that"

"Oh yes there is if someone accuses you of being a witch"

It now dawned on me their predicament. In this superstitious age this was a serious offence and the poor old woman's appearance would not help.

"Well you're safe with us we may believe in fate but none of this witchcraft rubbish"

She turned towards me.

"Thank you again young man, give me your hand"

Thinking she needed assistance to get up I offered her my hand. She took tight hold of it and looked at me as if she could still see.

"What's your name?"

"It's Bill Charlton"

"Well Bill you have a strong arm and a kind heart. At times one or the other of these will rule you. I hope you have the ability to select which one wisely"

"So do I" was all I could think of saying.

"Should I go on?" She asked

"Why not" What harm can it do I thought.

"Today your journey will change your life. Tragedy will give you a new home and family. The next time you travel this route it will be a path seeking revenge but it will lead you to a new name, life and love"

"What about love?"

Cubby could not help but ask

"That's in Bill's hands. All I know is the light will show the way"

She let go of my hand.

"I'm pleased to have met you. Fate will always be your friend"

We talked about nothing in particular for about half an hour before parting on our different journeys.

I would remember this old woman.

"Do you believe all that?" Cubby was sceptical

"Well she was right in that tragedy would give me a new family and home only it was in the past. We will have to wait and see if any of the rest turns out to be correct"

I was not sure if I hoped she was right or not but was reassured that fate was on my side. This distraction had slowed us down so we stepped up the pace for the rest of the journey.

We made a slight detour so I could pass what used to be my father's farm. I looked down upon it from the hillside as we approached. It looked familiar but run down. The tree outside the farmhouse was still there, I used to climb up it when I was young. The rope that I had tied to the main branch will have rotted away years ago. I used to swing as hard as possible then leave go to see how far I could jump. I would often fall flat on my face in the mud much to my father's annoyance. As my memories began to flood back a sadness fell over me. This was short lived as a young girl came running out of the house shouting.

"Mum there're some men coming"

"Come in Ella until I see who they are"

It was her mother my aunt Esther, John's widow and the child Ella I remembered as just a toddler.

We approached.

"We mean you no harm we're just passing through but would like to water the horses if you don't mind"

As she came up to me I recognised her but could tell she did not know who I was. I noticed her face was bruised and she had been bleeding from her lip.

"What happened?"

She did not reply but the little girl ran out and did.

"It was Little Willie Potts"

"He was beating my mother so I hit him with a stick and he punched me"

I noticed a black eye. I thought it must be a family trait this attacking people with sticks and branches.

"Who is he?" I asked.

"He is supposed to be renting what was my husband's farm and I am living here in his Brother William Charlton's house"

"Where are they?" I knew full well where they were but asked so as not to give away my identity.

"They have been missing six years and I am sure they're dead, but I have to wait seven years before its official"

"What should be done about Little Willie?"

"Nothing" was the reply "He is a dangerous man and not to be trifled with especially when he's been drinking"

"Is that where he is now?"

"Yes he's there now forcing people to buy him drinks which they do as they are all scared of him"

"Well Ella wasn't and neither am I"

"Then you should be" she warned.

"Come on Cubby I fancy a pint and you have the money" He looked at me and shook his head. As we left he looked around.

"With a bit of work this could be a good farm, will you be claiming it?"

"Don't know" I had other things on my mind. It was about time Little Willie picked on someone his own size and not little girls.

We took our time riding to Alwinton as I wanted to remember all the familiar places. They were all different when viewed from horseback. Some of the hedges I could not see over the last time I was here.

We eventually arrived at the inn. It was much larger than the alehouse we usually frequented. Out buildings formed three parts of a square, one was used for brewing ale and had barrels stacked against the wall the others provided accommodation for both men and horses. A number of men were gathered in the courtyard gambling by tossing pennies. They placed two pennies on a small piece of wood and threw them into the air. They would bet on either two heads, two tails or one of each. How the betting worked I was not sure but money changed hands frequently to much shouting and swearing.

"Come on Nebby" Someone shouted. "It's about time you got a pair of heads"

A rough looking lanky man was about to throw the coins. He had a huge nose which his narrow face exaggerated. It was obvious why they were calling him Nebby.

As they landed I heard a shout of "bugger" and assumed there were not two heads staring upwards. They were quickly picked up by a man I recognised; it was Walter Dodds the one who had taken ill that fateful day when I had accompanied my father. No wonder you lost I thought you must have used all the luck you had that day.

I then noticed Reverend Hall sitting on an upturned barrel watching the proceeding and drinking a tankard of ale. I had recognised him at once his dark hair was now trimmed with grey but this only seemed to enhance his good lucks. I wanted to shout out to him that I was alive but thought better of it.

I looked at Reverend Hall "Is the molester of women and little children inside?" I asked.

"That'll be Little Willie" he replied "Yes he's inside"

We dismounted and entered the inn. It was dark and dingy. The smell was overpowering it smelt like all ale houses but only much stronger. I thought either the ale was different or more likely the floor had not been swilled recently. I soon refocused my eyes and was able to spot the Innkeeper.

"Tell Little Willie I mean to kick his arse and see how he likes being picked on"

He hesitated, disappeared and no doubt passed on the message with some embellishments. It had the reaction I expected.

"He's going to do what" I heard shouted from the next room.

In charged Willie, he was the biggest bugger I had ever seen. I was six foot, but he was a head taller than me and twice as wide.

"Let's have no trouble in here" The Innkeeper commanded

"If you have any arguments take them outside"

So outside we headed. The gambling had stopped and the men were standing around the courtyard as if they had anticipated what would happen. I wondered if there was any money on me as it was obvious this was the new game.

Cubby suggested we had better run for it. But it was too late now. We squared up, but with a man this size I hadn't a clue what to do next. I did not need to worry he made the first move swinging a sword which crashed into a barrel almost splitting in halve. I only wanted to dish out a good thrashing but it had escalated into a fight to the death.

I danced around him parrying all his blows which only got him madder.

He howled "I'll cut you in halve you little bastard"

I dodged him again and pushed him back. He was unsteady on his feet and fell. As he tried to get up he grabbed the top of a barrel for balance. I slammed down my sword removing the finger ends on his left hand. He screamed dropped his sword whilst grabbing his hand. I kicked it away.

"Let that be a lesson"

I said with relief.

"Let everyone know that John Charlton's widow at Haugh farm is under my protection"

I turned away I had made my point. I did not notice Willie grab an onlooker's sword and charge at me from behind.

"Look out"

Cubby shouted and I immediately sensed the urgency of the call. I turned on my heal lashing out with my sword. It was an instinctive reaction which slashed open his throat and he fell gurgling to the ground. I had killed my first man even though I had not set out to do so.

"Serves him right"

I heard Reverend Hall comment.

"I have been expecting this for years"

Cubby threw down a purse to a spectator.

"If you clean up the mess and bury the body that's yours"

Our drinking money was gone so we mounted and turned for home.

"Who are you?"

Reverend Hall enquired.

"The prodigal son returned" I smiled "But no need to get out the fatted calve"

I sensed recognition in his eyes but could tell he was not sure.

"Keep the faith Reverend keep the faith"

As we moved away I heard someone ask him

"Well, who is he?"

"God knows; God knows" was his clever reply.

I had been lucky if Willie had been sober it might have been different. We later learnt that his name was not Willie at all but Harry and that being called Little Willie was not being ironic but was a nick name given to him as a child and referred to a particular part of his anatomy. I, on the other hand, had no name in Alwinton but speculation over it would soon spread.

It was a few days later at supper that James broached the subject.

"I hear there was a spot of bother at Alwinton the other day some stranger killed the local bully"

He looked straight at me.

"Know anything about it?"

"Probably some family quarrel" I avoided an answer.

"They say some warrior has appointed himself the protector of widows and children"

"Definitely sounds a family matter" I concluded.

"Maybe" He looked knowingly at me and smiled.

The matter was not pursued any further.

Little was I to know that my role as protector would soon change to bloody revenge. There were rumours spreading of a gang operating south of the border but close enough for us to be concerned. Cubby and I therefore travelled around the farm fully armed. On one of those days we had been checking cattle in the west field adjacent to Andrew Kerrs land. As we returned we could see a large number of men leading a herd of cattle past the farm. We stood on top of a hill looking down but out of sight. We could see James approaching them. Cubby dug in his spurs but before he could move I grabbed the reigns.

"There's nothing two of us can do let's just hope they pass peacefully by"

My hopes were dashed, the leader thrust a lance into James' chest and he fell to the ground. I knew he was dead. Ethel ran screaming from the house and tried to lift him up only to be struck with the flat side of a swords blade. She fell beside him unconscious.

"We must seek help we can't let them away with this" I gestured to Cubby.

"It's no good going to Matthews he can only raise five or six men and they must have at nearly fifty"

"We have to get Andrew Kerr he's deputy warden for the area and can call a hot trod"

We galloped off.

As we charged up to the farmhouse a girl was leaving, she spotted us, realised something was up and ran towards us.

"What's the matter Cubby?"

"We have terrible news Helen our farm has been raided; father is dead and maybe my mother as well"

"Dad is in the north pasture, if you get him I will round up as many men as I can"

We found him and relayed the full story.

"Let's get back to the house so I can collect my gear"

He was in a rage, reiving was bad enough but murder of one of his closest family friends was too much. As a senior member of the Kerr family and deputy warden of the middle March he had a duty to perform and was now sworn to do so.

When we got to the house half a dozen men were already fully armed awaiting Andrew's command.

"You six go off to the other farms, you know which ones they are, and bring back a many as you can I have called a hot trod so they will come"

"You say there are about fifty of them, do you know where they were heading"

"Yes, they were heading west up the valley, it's a large herd so they cannot be travelling quickly"

"Then we need to move in the next hour to catch them but the most men I can muster in that time will be no more than thirty"

"That may be enough" I suggested "I have an idea, if you wait until the river makes that long sweeping bend they will not be able to fight as well as keeping the cattle under control. They will not fight if there is nothing to gain and will probably just abandon them and try to make their escape by the drover's route into Upper Coquetdale "

"Then they will get away"

"Not if I can help it, just keep chasing them, and I will get the men there to arrange a greeting for them"

"That's the English side so why should they help?"

"This gang has more cattle than we had on our farm so they must have raided others on the way. We have called a hot trod and they will look bad if they ignore it when their kin have suffered"

"You could be right" Andrew agreed "And it's not as if we have a better plan"

He then instructed a couple of men who were too old to fight to attend to James and see how Ethel was.

"Right Cubby lets go"

So off we went.

"What's your plan Bill"

"Not sure, let's get some men first"

Alwinton was at the far end of the Upper Coquet so if we got there quickly we should be able to cut them off.

"There are sure to be men at the inn who could join us, or at least help us to raise a decent number"

"This is going to be interesting" Cubby smiled.

We got to the inn but it was quiet as there were no gamblers outside. I guessed that the toss penny crowd only met on certain days. We entered, it was surprisingly busy inside. Immediately a tall man recognised me, it was Nebby.

"Come to pick a fight again?"

"Well in a way I have, we have been raided and people killed so we have called a hot trod and are looking for men"

"Why should we get involved?" someone asked

"I'm sure they must have caused some damage in your valley, but if you want to stay here drinking and let others do your fighting you're going to be a soft touch for any future riders"

Reverend Hall then pushed forward.

"Yes, we have had two farms raided but fortunately the gang were spotted early enough for our people to get away, what do you intend to do?"

"Nothing unless I get some help"

"These are honourable men and will not ignore a hot trod when their people have been robbed and will help or they will be singled out for special mention on Sunday"

When Reverend Hall spoke I noticed people listened.

"How much time have we got?"

"We will have to move out in a couple of hours otherwise they will get away"

"What's the plan then?"

"Well that depends how many men we have"

"We can sort that out now" He called each man by name and after discussion concluded that in the time we had about twenty-five would be the number.

"Is that all?" was my surprised response.

"We could always bring our wives if it is only numbers you want" someone joked.

"That might not be as stupid as you think, can they ride"

"Of course, some of them as good as the men"

"I have an idea; do you think they could be mistaken for men from a distance?"

The comedian joked again," George's wife could be mistaken for a man real close up" George responded with "If we can catch them one by one your wife could shag them to death"

"Come on boys let's get serious"

"If we can get a dozen dressed like men holding broom shanks with knifes attached they could be mistaken for lancers if they don't get too close"

"We can manage with that" If we stick to my plan.

"Hold on a minute" the lanky guy butted in

"Who put you in charge; it should be one of our own"

"If it wasn't for me nothing would happen, I have a good plan and here" I cast my medallion at Reverend Hall.

It landed on the table spinning eventually settling face upwards.

He recognised it immediately.

"I thought it was you but wasn't sure, the prodigal son really has returned"

"Who is he?"

"He is one of us, its William Charlton's son from Haugh Farm" This seemed to satisfy their pride and they listened to my plan.

"Now you all know where to meet, but you must stay in the trees until I give the order else we could be in trouble"

"The women can meet in the same place; they don't need to worry they won't have to fight"

"Who will look after the bairns?" someone asked

"If you leave them at the inn Reverend Hall will look after them" I looked at him" You will won't you?" He nodded

"Any nursing mothers can stay and help as they have wee ones to look after"

I knew that if there were only twenty-five of us we could not tackle such a large number and needed to force them back towards Andrew and then attack them together. I needed to catch them in terrain that would suit us and make it difficult for them to escape. I knew the valley well especially where I hoped to set my trap. There was a narrow section where the walls were steep and rocky. Large rocks kept falling with such frequency that it was a waste of time trying to clear them. The result was an area of one or two hundred yards that was difficult to negotiate on horseback and impossible to fight whilst mounted. I meant to wait until they passed then show ourselves preventing them making a hasty retreat. I had calculated that by then Andrew and his men would be chasing directly behind them.

The Coquetdale men were as good as their word and arrived at the designated spot with almost thirty men and fifteen of their wives. The plan was straightforward but relied on good timing. It was now time to prepare. "Cubby, you take another two lancers with you and the women and ride up the rear of that hill here on the right. Stay just below the crest so as not to be seen and only you climb to the top to keep a lookout. When you see they have all passed the rocks. That's when you should show yourself, parade the three of you with lances first with the others behind. We will not move until we see you. Hopefully you will be mistaken for a sizeable force. I know you will not let me down, good luck"

With this he moved with his "lancers". As they rode the further away they got the more they looked like a formidable troupe. I picked two Robson brothers as my second in command and asked them to pick another dozen of the best fighters. We agreed that all of us would move forward out of the trees together for maximum impact. Then the fifteen of us would rush ahead to make initial contact. The rest would then back us up otherwise we might get in each other's way.

It was now a waiting game. It seemed to take forever but was probably no more than an hour before we heard them coming. It took them a while to wind through the rocks but I could tell they were in a hurry and I could see why. Andrew was on their tail and as they cleared the rocks he had dismounted and with his men was weaving on foot towards them. Cubby made his move and trotted his men in a line over the crest of the hill. They did look impressive and where spotted at once. That was when we moved out of the trees. The effect was immediate they realised they had fallen into a trap and panicked. About half of them abandoned their horses and tried to escape climbing up the rocky valley sides. We fifteen charged and the remainder of them headed back into the rocks. We leapt from our horses straight at them. The fight started on both fronts and we sandwiched them between us. The battlefield was no more than ten paces deep but ferocious. Some shots were fired on both sides but with little effect and as it was now hand to hand fighting it was impossible to reload.

I tackled the first man I met. I just rained blow after blow he just managed to parry them but my attack was so violent that he fell over one of the rocks. He tried to push himself up with his sword hand. I stepped on the sword crashing mine onto his helmet knocking him senseless onto the ground. I picked up his sword and charged forward swinging both of them.

A shot rang out and I saw Andrew hold his shoulder then lose his balance and fall. I ran to him just in time to block a sword with the one in my left hand and with the other I swung with such force I cleaved his attackers head clean off his shoulders. Andrew recovered and I stood back to back defending a man I had sworn to kill but had no time to ponder my dilemma. We were two big men and soon dispatched another two. There was a lull in our fighting and Andrew took the opportunity to leap onto a rock and shout at the top of his voice.

"Stop" and everyone seemed to pause to catch their breath "No one else needs die if you surrender your weapons" This coincided with the appearance of the other ten men and Cubby's lancers. They knew they were beaten and complied.

"Drop your swords" he commanded.

"Not you" I pointed at the man who had killed James "We have unfinished business"

Andrew interrupted "You don't need to do this; this is a legal hot trod we can just hang him"

"Yes I do"

He walked towards me carrying his sword he showed no fear and had an air of confidence.

I was so full of anger I never considered losing.

We clashed exchanging blows. I could feel he was strong and was soon to find out he was good as well. He manoeuvred me between two rocks which prevented me side stepping a stroke which slashed across my side. I felt the pain but it was not a disabling blow so I charged back with such force he lost his balance and before he could recover I slashed his throat and he fell forward gurgling and died in a pool of his own blood. I heard a loud cheer but could only think of Little Willie he had died exactly the same way. Serves the bastards right I thought.

Andrew came up to me "You really are a warrior until now James had been the best I have seen he has taught you well"

Cubby approached "He was my father I should have been the one to do that"

I thought of James and my eyes filled with tears.

"Mine as well"

Cubby paused then hugged me like friends meeting after a long separation.

"Sorry Bill, I should not have said that no one could have a better brother"

As the women attended to the wounded Andrew took charge.

"Take ten as hostage and give the rest enough horses for them to take the dead and wounded away"

Ten were tied together and forced to march all the way back while we rode. By the time we got to Andrews farm they were pushed exhausted into the barn.

"Leave them tied up and you four take turns to guard the door. If they need to go let them piss their pants if they haven't already"

With this he gestured to Cubby "Come on" and turned to me "You as well we've got wounds needing stitches"

I followed him into the house and this time took notice of his daughter. She was handsome rather than good looking with long brown hair and beautiful dark eyes. I quite fancied her. Cubby was behind me and when she saw him her eyes lit up. I knew they had been friends as children but it had now obviously developed into something much stronger.

"Get a needle and thread Helen, you have some stitching to do, see to him first then find a bed for them"

I stripped to the waist and she attended my wound. It was a long cut to my side but not too deep. As she stitched it hurt like hell but I tried not to show it. When she finished she covered it with a brown smelling paste. "What's that?" I enquired.

"Better you don't know" Andrew laughed

"But it does work"

While I was being attended to Cubby sought news of his parents. James had been killed outright. Ethel was still alive when they had got there but died soon after. She had insisted that they carried a message for us.

"I don't know if the boys could see what was happening but if they could let them know they did the right thing by keeping away. Tell them not to feel guilty there was no point in us all getting killed"

She died thinking of us.

The barn and house had been burnt and the cattle were gone.

They buried them together next to the house.

Two beds were made up for us and we settled down for the night. Neither of us could sleep. So we just talked. Or conversation got round to Andrew.

" Has he no sons?" I asked.

"He had three, the youngest died of the fever, the other during a reprisal raid, and Andrew doesn't talk about that"

"What about the eldest?"

"He died of his wounds the night we found you, that's his bed you're lying in"

This is getting too complicated; I was under the protection of the man who had killed my father, lying in the bed of his son who my father had killed, with my adopted brother who had killed my uncle.

Things couldn't get much stranger could they?

I now understand Andrews rage when he saw his son cut down and why he killed my father. My pledge to myself to kill him had festered so long I was no longer in control of my emotions. As I lay there I thought of the old woman. She had been correct, tragedy had brought me to a new home and family what I had thought was the past turned out to be the future. What else could she be right about?

Tomorrow is another day I thought knowing that the best chapter in my life so far had just ended. I had no idea what the future held.

Chapter Five
Andrew Kerr of Cessford

———

The next morning at breakfast we all sat around the table discussing the events.

"Before we can do anything we need to be fully aware of all the facts" Andrew was obviously concerned.

"We know we have lost one man in the fight and probably two from Coquetdale and counting James and Ethel that's a total of five, they have lost about the same. We need to confirm our losses as this will have a bearing on the ransom we demand. I will send out a couple of riders to make sure this is correct. This gang were from a number of families but their leader was an Elliot and that could be a problem"

Andrew left to organise the men.

We continued to eat breakfast and within minutes he joined us again.

"Cubby it's about time you and Helen sort yourselves out?"

"What do you mean?"

"It's obvious to everyone what is going on you cannot help keep looking at each other"

"I have been trying to pluck up the courage to ask your permission for her hand"

"You didn't ask permission for whatever the two of you were up to when you keep meeting in the barn"

Helen blushed and Cubby stammered "Err, err"

"Don't worry, even I was young once and I know your feelings are genuine otherwise I would have kicked your arse before now"

I knew then what Cubby's missing hours of solitude had been all about, no wonder he came back in such a good mood.

"Do you want to get married?" Andrew asked

"Yes" was their immediate joint reply.

"Good, but you should have asked before now" Andrew looked a Cubby.

Helen jumped to his defence "But you are rather intimidating"

Andrew laughed "And I don't intend to change; but it does simplify things, do you both agree to a handfastening until we can get a priest?"

They both smiled and held hands.

"That means you can share Helens room and Bill and I can have a room each" He paused.

" You now own James' farm and will inherit mine, so as the farms are adjoining it makes sense to run them both as one. There will be no need to waste time and money in rebuilding what has been burnt down"

That was it, all agreed, practical and sensible.

"We will sort out this Elliot matter tomorrow" was Andrews parting comment as if he had done enough for the day.

That evening at supper time we all sat around the table and Helen served the meal and then joined us. Andrew still looked pensive.

"We will have to meet the Armstrongs tomorrow and sort things out" He paused then continued

"The Elliots form a liaison with the Armstrongs who are the major family and as such are expected to support them. It is important that we resolve matters as they can muster some three thousand riders should they look for reprisals. This would be virtual war along the borders and I know they would not want this. Bill and I will set off first thing in the morning whilst Cubby can look after the hostages."

"Why me" I asked.

"I have my reasons" was the reply but he did not elaborate.

"What I can't understand is why they killed James or even why they passed by our farm, they could easily have avoided it and would have got clean away"

Cubby added "It appeared to be a deliberate attempt to kill my father as he did not provoke them, why do you think that was Andrew?"

"That's a long story" He replied "It stretches back long before either of you were born, in fact before James had met Ethel"

"Well go on" Cubby prompted.

Andrew began to explain that in his young days James had been a "warrior" and had built up a reputation as a great swordsman. So much so that he had met many challenges. They became almost sporting events and involved much gambling. Usually such challenges ended when the first blood was spilt.

One fateful day such an event had been arranged between James and one Thomas Elliot. It was to be on top of a hill where the old people had lived. It was an ancient site and all that was left was a circle of fallen stones which had obviously been a boundary wall. The circle was about fifty paces wide and formed a perfect arena. The fight had been preceded by numerous insults and much boasting by Elliot. James had responded to this by giving an exhibition of swordplay that totally embarrassed the opposition which culminated with a prod in the rear end drawing blood and thereby ending the contest.

As James was returning to his horse Elliot attacked from behind slashing his back. Fortunately, James still had his sword in his hand and managed to turn thrusting his sword deep into Elliot's chest felling him to the ground dead. His younger brother Mark ran at James who responded by kicking him soundly in the groin. This youngster was the Elliot who killed James and must have born a grudge for over twenty years. Andrew had helped James onto his horse and they both galloped off before matters could get any uglier.

Andrew knew he had to get help for James who could not make it all the way back home. They came across an isolated farm house well outside the Elliot territory. Andrew hammered on the door shouting for assistance. A young woman answered the door and immediately comprehended the situation. James was unconscious and together they dragged him onto a table to attend to his wounds. When they removed his jacket blood was still running freely.

"We have to stop this before it's too late if it isn't already" She was young but took command.

"Heat the poker in the fire while I stitch as best I can"

"I've done this to sheep before but never to a man, usually about half survive, I hope his odds are better"

The hot poker was applied it sizzled but the bleeding stopped immediately.

"Who is he?" she asked

"James Cessford"

"The swordsman, I've heard of him, is this the first time he has lost?" She queried

"He didn't lose; it was a cowardly attack from behind"

"Well I suppose if you're too good, and can't be bettered face to face, someone will eventually attack from behind if you play these dangerous games"

She was a beautiful young woman with long red hair and not very tall and could easily be taken for a child. But in all other respects she was mature and very capable.

"You will have to leave him here for a couple of weeks. Put his horse in the barn and he can ride it home once he recovers otherwise I will bury him close by"

"Thank you for attending to my friend I will leave him with you, I will return in a week or so, thank you again, oh by the way what is your name?"

"Ethel"

She was to nurse him day and night for the first few days and constantly thereafter. At the end of the third week he did ride home but not alone Ethel was to become his wife on condition that his days as a warrior were over.

"Well boys, that is the story so you can now understand why this terrible thing has happened and why James did not teach either of you fight until he thought you might be in danger".

"Let's get to bed there is a lot to do in the morning"

Next morning, we left early. It was one of those misty mornings were the clouds seemed to travel down the valley leaving the hills exposed. It gave a strange sense of foreboding a feeling which I dismissed like a bad dream. Andrew knew the way well and had no need to pause to check directions.

"Have you met John Armstrong?" Andrew asked not expecting an answer.

"He's an ugly bugger, but don't underestimate him for what he lacks in brains he more than makes up in cunning, thankfully he does keep his word so long as you don't give him an excuse not to"

We approached from the north following a small stream past what was obviously an old Roman fort. I could see the remains of the ditch which was shaped similar to a playing card, which is an oblong with rounded corners. I recalled Reverent Hall's description of them. We continued along the stream past a water fall turning south when we reached the river Esk. We then saw the house or more accurately Tower. This was Hollows Tower the home of John Armstrong; it was at least four stories high. At the top of the south gable there was a beacon not unlike a church belfry. It was an impressive building.

It was late afternoon before we arrived at the entrance. We were aware that there were lots of men around, many more than was needed to run a farm. It was obvious we had been expected. We were met by a stocky man who had a nasty scar to the left side of his face and wore a patch over that eye.

"Come this way" he demanded as he led us through the entrance.

"Wait a minute" Andrew paused

"Here Bill have a look at this" He pointed to the door.

I noticed spiral patterns carved into the sill.

"We have lots of these in Northumberland; they say they're made by the old people. My people treat them as being sacred and would not dare move them never mind use them to build with"

"May be" Andrew said

"But these are Armstrongs and fear neither man nor God"

I thought to myself they may not fear anyone but they have built a fortified tower with walls six foot thick.

The ground floor was a huge vaulted chamber where in bad weather cattle could be kept. A spiral staircase wound clockwise to the main room on the next floor.

"Careful of the next step" We were warned.

It was a trip step out of sequence with the others there to trip any attacker rushing up the stairs. A good idea I thought as anyone falling foul of it and being killed or injured would block the narrow staircase.

As we entered the main room it was surprisingly light. Two arched windows on the East and West walls were obviously designed to get the best of morning and evening sunlight. John Armstrong was sitting at the end of a long table. He gestured for us to take a seat. I could see they knew each other.

"This is a fine mess you have got us into Andrew"

"Maybe but it was not of my making" Andrew responded without any hint of apology.

"But you have killed a couple of Elliots from a family I am sworn to protect"

"Protect yes, but not condone cold blooded murder against a family with which you have a long standing truce"

"I am still expected to resolve the matter without the Elliot's loosing face. If I was to demand the release of the hostages without ransom this would help as no one gains anything and the dead on each side just about balance out" John Armstrong looked as if he was hiding a smile with his demand.

"I have my family interests as well and with four widows need the ransom to recompense them"

Armstrong got annoyed "I can raise 3000 riders and come and get them without paying a penny"

"Then you will be outnumbered, I have my family and associates and as they offended the Robsons of Coquetdale who are allied with the Charltons and Robsons of Tynedale. You will not be able to count the widows on each side"

"Charltons, they won't get involved?"

"Well they have family in Coquetdale who were also affected and feel they can't ignore their obligations; this is Bill Charlton with me to represent them"

I now knew why I was here.

"He could be anyone" Armstrong was shouting

At this I tossed my medallion on the table it bounced but he caught it before it could hit the table again. I was not sure if he could read the inscription but he recognised the Charlton crest.

"Neither of us wants to come to blows over this matter, we have to find a compromise"

I could see that this was the position that Andrew had been angling for. He paused as if thinking then made his offer.

"We need the ransom but recognise we need your cooperation so I think it is only fair that we should share it equally"

I could see immediately that Armstrong liked the idea of getting something out of it.

"I think this would resolve the ransom matter but there is still another issue" Armstrong went on.

"The Elliots are unhappy that your man still killed Mark after you stopped the fighting saying no one else need die, they want you to hand him over"

"I can't do that he was not a Kerr and this would only provoke another family into getting involved"

Armstrong scratched his head, he obviously had an idea.

"Then can I make a suggestion"

He paused then continued.

"If they want him let them send one of their men to face him man to man and we can all agree that this will be an end to the matter, unless your man hasn't the stomach for it"

"That's fine with me" I interrupted.

"It was you" Armstrong was surprised "Best not to mention he's a Charlton"

"Well if that's everything agreed we will go. Once we have received the ransom we can arrange the duel but each side can only have ten men in attendance. Where shall we hold it?"

Armstrong smiled "The usual place where the old people lived"

"Come on Bill lets go home" As we left Andrew asked quietly "What about your wound"

"We have a few days yet I am sure it will have healed enough by then"

"I think they have caught a Charlton lion by the tail God help them when it turns"

He put his hand on my shoulder and I sensed respect.

"I hope I don't have to fight that one eyed man he would frighten the dead"

"You mean Wanless, that's what they call him, it means unlucky you know" Andrew smiled.

"But they always say it as 'one less' because he only has one eye and the daft bugger does not realise it"

It was three days before John Armstrong arrived with the money that had been agreed. He came alone and after the hostages were released he and James divided the ransom. It was obvious Armstrong was keeping the money for himself but Andrew was committed to dividing it between the widows although there was nothing to force him.

Armstrong turned to me.

"The Elliots say they will be ready in three days; can I say you are in agreement with this"

"That's fine with me so long as it puts an end to the matter"

Andrew butted in "Remember only ten men on each side can attend"

Armstrong mounted his horse

"We did not agree a time, is mid-day all right?"

I nodded and Andrew replied "We will be there"

As Armstrong rode away Andrew looked straight at me.

"Everything is all right isn't it?"

Andrew seemed genuinely concerned.

"Yes I just wish it was all over, but don't worry I will not be losing any sleep over it"

He continued "I smell a rat, I just don't trust the Elliot's they're up to something, we had better post lookouts in case they ignore the ten men agreement"

I was beginning to respect this man he was nobody's fool and certainly stood by his family and friends. To my surprise this seemed to include me.

The next couple of days dragged especially as Andrew would not let me do any farm work in case my wound reopened and he had assigned Cubby the duty of making sure I didn't. He had a long talk with me as to who we should take in attendance. He and Cubby were first on the list and I suggested the Robson brothers from Coquetdale and Reverend Hall just in case. I was happy for Andrew to select the remainder so long as one of them knew how to treat wounds, again just in case.

The day finally arrived and we gathered for the ride up to the designated place. Andrew came out carrying something wrapped up in a towel. He handed it to me.

"I had this made especially for my son it has perfect balance and is much better than yours, I have no need for it now, but it would please me for you to use it in what I see as a matter of family honour"

I opened up the parcel. It was the most beautiful sword I had ever seen; it was ornate and had the chevron with the three stars of the Kerr family crest enamelled on the hand guard. The blade was sharp and had engraved just below the hilt what looked like a face in the shape of the sun; again this was part of the coat of arms.

"You honour me, I will be proud to use it"

We arrived at the site ahead of the Elliots which was Andrew's idea. We waited until we could see them heading up the hill. Andrew placed his hat on his lance and held it in the air. I noticed the same reply from two distant hills.

"They have only brought ten men with them maybe I have maligned them unfairly"

At this Andrew moved forward to greet the party.

John Armstrong shook his hand.

"It would be a shame to waist the opportunity for a wager; I will put a couple of pounds on my man unless that is too strong for you"

"Let's make it five" was Andrew's response "I have seen my man fight"

"Good, then let the two men step forward"

A tall red headed man stepped forward. He looked calm had no hint of an expression and did not say a word. I stood in front of him and looked straight into his eyes. He did not blink.

Armstrong seemed to be organising the event.

"Take a step back each of you and when I drop my hat commence, remember this is a fight to the death and does not end with first blood"

"We did not agree to this" Andrew protested but he was too late the hat had already hit the ground.

Elliot or who I assumed was an Elliot swung his sword at knee height and then brought it straight up. I managed to parry it just below the hilt of my sword. I was only the length of my hilt from losing my arm. This was a move even James had not taught me. I swung back at him and the swords clashed sparks flying. I could tell my strength had surprised him as his skill had me. I forced him backwards towards the old walls. He resisted my advance parrying all my blows. Then when blocking one of my high strokes he spun around quickly on his heal almost removing my head with a backhand sweep of his sword. I had ducked just in time but managed to clip his left hand.

Andrew shouted out "That's first blood let that end it"

His comments were totally ignored in fact the fight seemed to intensify. We moved back and forward covering almost the whole area within the old stone circle. I was younger and had expected him to tier but he was hardly panting. The sweat was now running down my arm but thankfully my sword grip was still dry. He spun round again this time rattling his blade against my hand guard. This was the third time he had tried to attack my sword arm. I now realised that this must be his favourite move as any attempts at my body would be riskier as it would leave my sword arm free. He was obviously trying to disable me then go in for the kill. I now knew I had to change tactics this man was too good and sooner or later I would make a mistake.

Our swords locked yet again giving me time to butt him in the face. He fell backwards with blood pouring from his nose.

"You bastard I'll kill you for that" he screamed.

This was the first sound he had made and it immediately gave away his accent. He was no Elliot in fact not even from the borders.

"It's Jock Campbell" one of Andrew's men shouted

"I thought I recognised him"

Andrew had been right not to trust the Elliots they had contracted the Scottish Champion.

This made me angry. I remembered James' teachings he always said it didn't matter how you fight so long as you win. He was not just a swordsman he was a fighter, and fight is what I must do. The next time our swords locked I raised my knee into his groin. He stepped back giving me room to follow that blow with a full blooded kick. As he fell to his knees I crashed my sword onto his helmet. Still dazed he tried to stand only to fall backwards onto the crumbling wall. In his eyes I could see a combination of both anger and surprise. Before he could recover his senses I plunged my sword into his chest.

There was silence for a moment then a great cheer from my supporters. Andrew smiled

"I think you owe me five pounds"

Armstrong threw a purse onto the ground turned and left without further comment.

"Come on Bill let's go"

Andrew put his hand on my shoulder.

An Elliot commented "Is that your son, we thought he was dead?"

"If he isn't then why is he sleeping in my Son's bed?"

Andrew's clever response seemed to satisfy everyone. As the Elliots had fielded an impostor he was keen not to be accused of doing the same. John Armstrong kept quiet as he was happy for the matter to be closed and to keep secret his share of the ransom.

"Thank God it's all over" I looked at Andrew.

"Not quite there is the drinking now" he was laughing "I think I can afford to supply the ale"

"I hope you are not offended at them thinking you are a Kerr but it was necessary"

"It was an honour" was all I could think of saying.

We headed for the first Ale House within the safety of the Kerr's territory.

Cubby borrowed pipes from the landlord and we sang and drank until the early hours. James and Ethel's death was forgotten but only for that evening.

Next morning at breakfast there was little conversation. This was not the result of the Ale but more the effect of ending one chapter but not being quite ready for the next one. Then Andrew joined us.

"Here" he said handing Cubby and I each a small leather purse "The ransom is to be divided between the widows which includes Ethel, I am sure she would have wanted me to share it between you"

"I'm sure she would" Cubby confirmed

Cubby and I were charged with taking the Coquetdale widows share of the ransom. I was looking forward to this as things would be different now that they knew who I was.

My first call was at Haugh Farm to see Esther.

She had spotted me coming and was waiting at the door. She looked apprehensive.

"Come to claim your inheritance have you?"

"I haven't decided what to do yet, can I come in and talk about it"

We sat at the table. The room looked clean but I could see some repairs were needed as with the farm in general. She was still unsure of my intentions.

"Now you have confirmed John is dead as the only male heir you can claim both John and your father's farms"

"That may be the law, but it isn't right" I knew what my father would have wanted.

"What I intend to do is claim both farms so they come under my protection but allow you to continue to live here. When Ella eventually marries, John's farm will be my wedding present. My father's farm I will occupy only if I ever need to; does that sound reasonable?"

"You're a good man Bill"

I thought for a moment.

"Not really" I replied "But I do know what is right; here" I handed over half the ransom money I had received. "Use this to get the repairs done and if there is any leftover spend it on yourself and Ella"

"You really are a good man" She got up hugged me and kissed me on the cheek.

"Well I have to look after my inheritance"

I tried to make light of the matter.

"Where are you off to now?" She enquired

"I'm going to find the Robson brothers so they can pay the ransom money to the widows"

"You need not look far when they passed before they were off to the Ale House at Alwinton to continue celebrating your victory"

"Well we had better not waste any time in case we miss them" Cubby said smilingly

Then Ella came skipping in.

"Ella this is your cousin Bill"

"Are you really my cousin?" She questioned

I nodded, she smiled and skipped away.

"Great, wait till I tell my friends. You're famous you know"

We all laughed as we were departing.

"Famous eh!" Cubby kept repeating as we rode to Alwinton.

As we approached the inn we could hear it was busy. I entered unnoticed at first and looked for a seat while Cubby went for the ale. I was noticed by Nebby who was the main objector to me taking command last time.

"It's Bill" He called out

"Come on I will buy you a pint, I assume your friend will want one as well"

At least four people stood up and offered me a seat.

I declined and squeezed in on a long bench that ran along the rear wall of the room.

Nebby returned holding a pint in each hand.

"Here you are, I'm Harry and I'm related to the Robsons so in some way I must be a relative of yours as well"

"That's good you will be able to tell me if you have seen the Robson brothers"

"They're in here somewhere, probably in the back after all the ale they have drunk. If it's business you need to discuss I would wait until tomorrow"

"Good idea" Cubby interrupted "It will be dark soon so we might as well stay the night"

Harry queried "I hear the Elliots were calling you Bill Kerr why was that"

I thought before answering.

"Andrew Kerr had a son called Bill and with me staying in his house I think that has caused the confusion, maybe it's a good idea to let them think that then none of the families on Coquetdale will be at risk from the Elliots"

"You're probably right, but you are definitely one of us tonight, so let us enjoy our celebrations"

I could not spend any of my money that night. Only a couple of weeks ago no one knew who I was and now it appeared almost everyone in the inn was related to me one way or another.

The men were genuine and I liked them. They lived in hard and often dangerous times and rarely had anything worth celebrating. One of theirs had killed the Scottish champion which to them was a major event. I did not fully appreciate it at the time but it was also a significant event for me, not only was I an adopted Kerr, it brought a reputation which would have an important influence on my future.

The Robson brothers eventually joined us but by this time did not talk any sense. I took Harry's advice and agreed to leave my business until the next day.

"How are you related to the Robsons?"

Cubby was interested.

I explained that the Robsons and Charltons are two major families living in Tynedale. That is how my grandfather met his wife who was a Robson. There were also a number of Robsons who years ago had settled in Coquetdale. My grandmother's father was a distant relation of one of them and eventually inherited a farm in Coquetdale. When she married my grandfather they left Tynedale and took over that farm which had been given to them as a wedding present. They had two Sons John and William. When my grandparents died the farm was split into two between the two brothers as was the custom. My father married a Coquetdale Robson so I am more Robson than Charlton.

"Thanks" Cubby replied "I am sure I won't remember any of that in the morning, wish I had never asked"

"He's one of us" George Robson just about managed to say as he tried to pat me on the back but didn't quite make it as he fell unconscious on the floor where he spent the night. No one bothered to move him and he just became another obstacle as people came back and forwards filling their tankards. The number of obstacles grew as the night progressed. Thankfully Cubby and I never joined them as we finished the night sleeping on the long bench.

Next morning, we managed to wake George Robson and complete our business. He would have the unpleasant duty of paying the widows. Ransom was a normal business transaction paid by the family of men captured during raids or in this case those caught during a Hot Trod. There was no obligation on the part of the capturers to pass any of the money on but as Andrew had given his word no one dare do otherwise.

As I was about to leave the inn George's brother Percy entered.

"There is someone outside wants to speak to Bill. She looks like a witch to me"

Could it be the blind old woman again I thought? If it was I would pay more attention to what she says this time. It wasn't it was someone dressed in dirty tattered clothes.

"I'm Bobby's mother can you tell me what happened to him. I know you were with him the night he disappeared"

This could be awkward. I would have to perpetuate the story about the Kerrs finding me with a broken leg but needed to give her some explanation.

"Yes I was. He was shot and died immediately so he did not suffer. I managed to ride away but in my panic lost control of my horse and fell. I lay there quietly until I was found next morning"

I hoped this would give her some comfort.

"He wasn't the best of sons but he was all I had after his father died. He did help to support me on the few occasions when he had not wasted all his money"

I felt sorry for the old woman as I watched her slowly walk away. George then explained to me that she had lost her cottage due to non-payment of rent and that her only income was from cleaning and sowing. The Reverend Hall let her sleep in one of the church's outbuildings normally used to store firewood. Most of the villagers help when they can but she still leads a meagre existence. She occupied my thoughts as we rode away.

On returning to what was now our home we settled down to the business of running what was now a fairly large farm. Andrew or course was very much in charge and handled all the finances including our wages. We were well paid, much more than the average farm worker, but in keeping with what family members would be paid. We worked hard which helped forget the recent past but memories would flood back once we were not occupied or met anyone who had been involved.

Andrew as Deputy Warden was often at Cessford Castle the home of Sir Walter Kerr Warden of the March. On his return on one of these occasions he asked for our assistance. It was nearing the time for a Truce Day and it was Andrew's duty to ensure that proper notice was given. On the Truce Day the Wardens of the Middle Marches of England and Scotland would meet at a predetermined place to hear Bills issued by inhabitants of one country against the other. It was therefore a formal legal hearing conducted under Border Law. Andrew was keen to show that he took his duties seriously and had asked Cubby and I to accompany his messenger to ensure things were carried out properly.

It was a day out for us. We visited all the local villages and supervised the messenger who would sound a horn in centre of each village and wait until a reasonable number of villages gathered around. He then read out the notice giving the town of Yetholm as the meeting place with the date being July 5th. Surprisingly everyone seemed interested and looked forward to what was considered a social event. At the last village we quenched our thirst in the Ale House before heading home after what for us had been an easy day's work.

July the 5th happened to be a cloudy but dry day with sunny intervals so visibility was quite good. As we approached Yetholm people seemed to be arriving from all directions and gathering in a large field on the North side of the town. We met up with Sir Walter Kerr and his son yet another William. He was young; I guessed less than 20, too young yet to be Deputy Warden but destined to eventually take over from his father. Andrew was therefore considered to a more appropriate deputy, at least for the moment.

We waited for the arrival of the English contingent. They would pass Windy Gyle on route to Yetholm along the drover's road one of the main routes between England and Scotland. As they made their way down hill they stopped about half way. Sir John Forster the English Warden dispatched his Deputy who rode up to us.

"Can you give assurance that you agree to uphold the Truce until the rising of the sun tomorrow"

Walter replied "I do" and raised his hand so as to be clearly seen by Forster.

"Can you now obtain the same assurance from your side?" Walter asked purely to conclude the formalities knowing it would be granted.

"I will" the Deputy replied and then headed back up the hill.

Forster dually raised his hand and they all moved towards us.

People were still arriving, so many it would be difficult to count accurately. I guess there were about three thousand in all, roughly divided equally between the Scottish and English. For these occasions with the Wardens present there should have been a limit of one thousand a side. No one bothered to count or even acknowledge that the rule applied.

Most of the people were not at all interested in the legal matters but mingled around what was almost a village of stalls. It was like a market and fair all rolled into one. We could smell hogs roasting on spits; ale was available from a huge cart that had struggled to get into the field. Nevertheless, we had business to attend to and those involved gathered together away from these distractions.

It being the first meeting after midsummer there were a number of formalities dictated by Border Law. The Wardens were required to take an oath. Walter stepped forward, took a bible from the clerk and read out most impressively. He swore to.

"Carry out his office without respect of person, malice, favour or affection"

He went on to state he would do all in his power to deliver "true offenders".

This done Sir John Forster followed suite.

Andrew looked at me and smiled. I knew what it meant. Oaths had been sworn by two of the biggest rouges in the border. If they were not directly involved with most of the cross border raids they would have profited from them or have been paid to look the other way.

It was now time for Walter to pick six good men of standing and to exclude any "infamous persons." He picked two Kerrs, one Cessford and one Ferniehirst, and another four from other major families. Forster likewise picked six men on the English side. These would be the jury for the following year. The two Wardens then moved to one side to discuss the bills that had been issued. They agreed on ten bills to be heard that day and would listen to them in the order of the latest first.

The first bill was a Hall who had accused a Cranston of stealing four cows. Hall had to first swear an oath as to the value of the cattle having "been sold all at once in market at the time of taking". Unfortunately for Hall some of the Cranstons were related by marriage to the Kerrs.

After deliberation no consensus could be reached and the case was not proven. I could not help thinking that all the trouble in arranging this Truce Day and all the formalities that I had just witnessed were purely for show and that no real justice would take place today. Except when families of no consequence were involved and decisions could be made without any serious offence.

Having no involvement with the proceedings Cubby and I headed for the stalls. A pint of ale and the smell of that roasting hog were too tempting for us. We passed stall after stall selling almost anything. Trade between England and Scotland was not encouraged; in fact, trade in items such as weapons and horses were strictly illegal with heavy punishments. A Truce Day was therefore the ideal opportunity to buy and sell.

I noticed a stall selling bracelets and necklaces; they were dangling from a rail and glinted with the sun. I had to raise my hand to shade my eyes from the reflected sunlight. A girl was trying on a necklace of bright blue glass beads. I could only tell she was a girl by the way her hair had been tied back. She wore trousers and carried both a sword and dirk the only weapons allowed on truce days.

As I approached her to satisfy my curiosity she turned and looked straight at me. It stopped me in my tracks. She was beautiful with bright blue eyes which framed by her red hair gave her an angelic look. I stammered.

"With those eyes you do not need glass beads"

She smiled and looked at Cubby.

"Who is this idiot?"

She enquired in a way to suggest she was not the least bit interested.

"He's my brother Bill, but don't worry he is usually quite harmless" Cubby was enjoying the way she had dismissed me.

I was too busy looking at her I had not noticed John Ferniehirst come from behind. He pushed me to the side.

"Keep away from my sister" He commanded

"Mary, keep away these Cessfords they are nothing but trouble"

As he turned and glared at me I noticed a scar above his right eye where I had hit him with the hilt of my sword.

"I will not break the truce but one day I will repay you"

At this he grabbed Mary by the arm and led her away.

"Stop slavering Bill she is not available. You certainly have a knack of finding trouble. Come on let's have that pint".

"Yes let's" It was not difficult to agree with Cubby's suggestion so we headed off.

"Well at least I know her name"

"That will be a great comfort to you on a cold winter night" Cubby mocked me.

There was something about this woman I could not forget even dressed the way she was her beauty still shone out. Then it dawned on me she was the girl who had shot me years before now fully grown. Little did I know we would soon meet again under less pleasant circumstances. Next time she would remember me.

Chapter Six
Mary Kerr of Ferniehirst

A ndrew asked Cubby and I to deliver a letter to the land agent in Jedburgh. It was necessary to formalise the change of the rental agreement for the small piece of land to now be in favour of Cubby rather than James. It was a bright sunny day so we decided to take a more scenic route. We crossed the hills with the intention of reaching the river Jed and following it into the town. This was a remote area, and a route not normally taken, so we did not expect to meet anyone not even a Ferniehirst whose territory we were crossing. At least that's what I hoped as I had got shot at the last time I took a similar route.

As we approached the brow of a hill we could see a wisp of smoke rising from a clearing in the trees. In case they were Ferniehirsts we dismounted so as not to be seen. We observed several men sitting around a fire cooking what seemed to be a lamb on a wooden spit. On the edge of the clearing we could see someone tied to a tree with what must have been their horse tethered to the same tree. Cubby had the eyesight of an eagle and spotted that the prisoner looked like a young man as he was small and had a mop of red hair.

"It's Mary Ferniehirst"

"It could well be" I agreed "But what is going on?"

"They must be outlaws probably from the debatable lands south west of here; they must have been looking for cattle and come across Mary"

"I guess you are right, and it is a lot easier and more rewarding to take her for ransom rather than have the bother of driving a few head of cattle; what should we do Cubby?"

"Nothing, if we get involved these things never turn out as you expect and the Ferniehirsts will not like being beholding to us"

"We can't do nothing, after all it is a woman on her own and she must be terrified"

Cubby looked at me, shook his head.

"Bill your honour will be the death of one of us sooner or later"

I laughed and joked "Hope it's not me then"

"Well Bill what's the plan?"

"I am sure I can skirt around this hill and get to the river undetected then using the bank as cover I can get to the edge of the clearing. As they have conveniently left her horse with her it would not take me long to release her and make an escape"

"I will only need a few seconds so if you can come from the other direction and distract them it should be easy"

Cubby smiled "As simple as that, but I will need a signal when you are ready"

"I will raise my handkerchief; it should only take me half an hour to get into position but maybe a little longer for you"

Cubby agreed and pointed to the right of their camp.

"In that case I will show myself beside that large oak tree but for only a few seconds, and then wait for the signal"

"Afterwards we will meet at the old bridge"

We nodded to each other as we retreated back down the hill then rode off in opposite directions.

The bright sunny day was now a problem as visibility was good and I had to be careful not to be spotted. I rounded the hill and was fortunate that a small copse of trees growing at its base allowed me to reach the river undetected. I rode my horse slowly in the shallows for as far as I could but eventually had to dismount and lead him. I managed to get within fifty yards of Mary and tethered my horse. The camp was only twenty yards from the river so I crept along the bank side. At that point the river was running fast creating quite a roar which I hoped would hide any noise I might make. It was damp causing me on one occasion to slip and slide towards the water I just managed to grab an overhanging branch. I scared a couple of wood pigeons which took to the air flapping noisily. Thankfully no one considered this to be unusual. I was lucky to eventually hide only yards away concealed by a large bush. I parted the branches carefully a have a good view of the situation.

I kept quiet as one of the men approached Mary. I felt helpless and could only hope she would be alright.

He walked up to her grabbed her blouse and ripped it open exposing both her breasts.

"Just checking out the merchandise"

He laughed. Mary spat in his face "You cowardly bastard it takes seven of you to catch one woman"

He raged "I think I will stick you one"

"I suppose an ugly bugger like you could only have a woman when she is tied up."

Mary showed her contempt.

He slapped her hard across the face and I could see a trickle of blood from her nose. She licked it away with her tongue and glared at him. She showed no sign of fear but must have been terrified; what a brave girl I thought.

"Leave her alone" someone shouted

"We don't want to reduce her value; but you can sit there and keep an eye on her"

"And you" He said pointing to another

"You can join him to make sure he behaves himself"

This was not what I wanted to hear it was going to be more difficult now. I had hoped to release her without the use of violence but this would now be impossible.

Fortunately, they sat with their backs to me facing Mary. This allowed me to try to catch her attention. It seemed she would never look my way but eventually she did. I raised my finger to my lips and could tell she knew I was there to help.

I now had to wait for Cubby to show himself.

We exchanged glances several times. On a couple of occasions, I detected a smile which was confirmation that I was doing the right thing in rescuing her. I could not help looking at her almost to the point of forgetting to watch out for Cubby.

I looked up just in time to see Cubby show himself. I waited a few moments to ensure the two guards were not looking my way and raised my handkerchief.

We had not planned exactly how he would distract them but I soon found out.

There was a shriek of pain as one of the men jumped up trying to pull an arrow out of his rear end. Another arrow struck a nearby tree. Mary's guards were distracted and focussed on the commotion so I managed to free her hands but as I did so could not help gazing at her beautiful milk white breasts. I handed her my dirk so she could cut her feet free as I got her horse.

Her guards who had been momentarily distracted now realised what was happening turned. I drew my sword and tackled them. I forced one backwards but the other tried attack me from behind. Before I could react Mary charged at him.

"Stick me would you" She shouted and plunged the dirk into him." See how you like it"

An arrow then struck the other in the shoulder and he ran to take cover.

I let him go then lifted Mary onto her horse smacking its hind quarters. She galloped off and I ran to get my horse and followed.

The others were still trying to hide from the arrows and were afraid to cross the clearing to give chase but Cubby was now long gone.

I ran towards the river and slid down the muddy bank into the water, it was shallow so did not slow me down too much. I reached my horse and chased after Mary who was now well ahead and at full gallop just off the bank side of the river. I rode for a couple of miles before almost catching her up. I was only yards away when her horse hit a rabbit hole and fell heavily; Mary leapt out of the saddle and followed the horse as they rolled down the bank. Her quick thinking saved her life as she had to avoid the horse or it would surely have crushed her.

The bank side was at this point about thirty feet high with a steep rocky slope to the river. The horse was crying out in agony and Mary was lying quiet at the bottom. I grabbed my sword ran down to the stricken animal and plunged it into its chest killing it at once in case the noise gave away our position.

I ran to Mary, she was pale and in obvious pain.

"Are you badly hurt?"

"Yes" She replied wincing with pain.

"My leg and arm are broken I heard the crack"

I could see her leg was misshaped and knew I had to straighten it out otherwise it could cause lasting damage.

"I will have to get some splints I will not be long"

Trees lined the river so I easily lobbed off some branches with my sword.

I cut the reigns off the dead horse to strap up both her leg and arm. Her arm was not so much a problem although broken it was not misshaped like her leg.

"Mary I have to straighten out your leg before I can splint it, it's going to hurt like hell but try not to shout out"

"I know so just get on with it as the thought of it has me petrified"

I had to pull her leg to line it up with the other one. I could tell she was in agony by the grimace on her face but she never made a sound. My admiration for this woman grew. I had liked her even when she had shot me and could not get her out of my mind since I saw her on the truce day, but that was only infatuation; it was now the real thing.

My actions had reduced the level of the pain but I could see she was still seriously hurt.

I could hear a horse coming and prayed it was Cubby. He had noticed my horse and guessed something was wrong.

"Bill" he shouted.

"Down here" I replied "Mary is badly hurt and there is no way she could ride a horse"

"Then we are in trouble, if they are reasonable trackers they will eventually follow you here" Cubby was planning something.

"If I hide my tracks and ride off with the two horses they may follow thinking the tracks are yours and Mary's"

"Yes but it will be obvious that we stopped here and they will wonder why"

"I thought of that and will give them a reason for stopping"

At this Cubby dropped his trousers and deposited a large turd on the ground.

"I was desperate to do that any way"

He finished off using a hand full of grass.

"You had better cut some more branches to hide the horse and yourselves until I get help; if you think it is safe and you are able to travel I will meet you at the old bridge as planned otherwise I will look for you along the river bank; I could be a while as I intend to lead them well away from here"

I did as I was told. I propped Mary up against the dead horse and covered us all up with branches.

We lay there quietly for a while before hearing horses approaching. They stopped and dismounted just above us. We dare not look but listened carefully.

"They have stopped here but I don't know why" we heard someone say.

Then another cried "Ah! Shit" He had stood on Cubby's deposit.

"So that's why he stopped; he will do more than mess himself if we catch him"

Their tracker then commented "Look they have headed off this way see this horse's tracks are still deepest and the other carries a lighter weight; come on we still might catch them".

We heard them ride off.

Well done Cubby I thought he even had the sense to ride my horse.

"Look Mary, we cannot stay here in case they realise what has happened and return"

"I am sorry but I cannot walk at all; you go and get my brothers and let us hope they don't find me"

"It's only a mile to the bridge and you are not very heavy so I will carry you"

I stood her on one leg and placed her good arm around my neck and lifted her. I was right she wasn't very heavy, at least not yet.

She was in pain and I dare not keep putting her down and lifting her up again so I carried her all the way.

At first it was easy there was a flat narrow strip of turf next to the river but it soon became a choice of proceeding in the river or attempting to climb the steep river bank. I elected to walk along the shallow edge of the river as I was afraid I might otherwise fall. This option became increasingly difficult as the large rocks in the river were smooth and slippery. I struggled on until I reached a point in the bank where it was not too steep and managed to clamber up. It was easy going now but we were no longer hidden from sight. It took me over an hour to cover this one mile and when we reached the bridge I was totally exhausted.

"I know Cubby will check here first so we will hide under the bridge"

I made her comfortable and sat beside her.

She began to shiver which I knew was a danger signal and that I must keep her warm. I took off my jacket and we huddled together using it as a blanket. She looked at me as if wanting to object but knew it was for her benefit.

Although it as a sunny day, under the bridge next to a cold stream it was quite chilly. I was concerned and knew it was best not to let her sleep so I tried to keep her awake with constant talking. We talked about the feuding between the Kerrs of Ferniehirst and those of Cessford. Mary explained that each family thought they were the more senior and that they should hold the position of Warden of the Middle March. Currently it was held by Sir Walter Kerr of Cessford much to the annoyance of the Ferniehirsts. This rivalry was deep rooted and in the past had resulted in murders by both sides.

She then enquired, "Bill, why did you help me?"

She had spoken my name for the first time and I must admit I liked it. I tried to make light of her question.

"Well, you were a damsel in distress and we men are duty bound to come to the rescue"

"Don't be silly, you are no Knight in shining armour"

"Maybe not but I am all you have at the moment"

"Yes you are, but your rescue has hardly gone to plan, I may have come to less harm if you had let them ransom me"

I laughed "That's exactly what Cubby warned would happen"

She laughed as well.

"You are lucky to have a brother like Cubby he is very loyal"

"Yes I know but we will not let him know that"

"Well you should, I wish my brothers got on as well as you two seem to. You know you look nothing alike and you are much bigger than Cubby"

She had inadvertently forced me into an explanation.

"Well, we're not real brothers you know but it is easier to call us that otherwise it gets too complicated"

This had certainly stimulated her curiosity

"Complicated? That's just what I need to take my mind off the pain and if it's not too boring it would prevent me going to sleep as well "

She was right and although I did not know her well I found it easy to pour out my whole life's history. She listened with interest and I could tell her attitude towards me was changing.

She laughed "Being rescued by a Cessford is bad enough so we had better not mention you are English as well"

"Go on tell me more and make it funny to take my mind off the pain"

"Alright then I will tell you about our great fishing escapade. This bridge reminds me of the one we should have taken."

It was a hot summer's day, a time of year when lambing was finished, the crops were all planted, and the cattle grazed without needing feeding. After the cows had been milked James came up to us.

"You boys should take advantage of such a day and go fishing, I will get Ethel to put some food together and join you later"

We needed no persuading we grabbed our rods and headed off. Our rods were not fancy, only a pole with a line about twenty feet long, but good enough to laze on a bank side dangling them in the river. This is exactly what we did, at least for a while.

"You know we will never catch a fish here in the direct sun light, we need some shade. Look there is the perfect spot"

Cubby pointed to the other side of the water where a large willow tree hung over the river.

"No way am I swimming across there, I know its summer but that river's always cold"

I was adamant.

Cubby thought for a while.

"What we need is a boat, wait a minute I know the perfect thing; we will get one of the cattle troughs. We use them for water when there's a dry spell so they must be water tight"

"That's a good idea Cubby"

Mary interrupted me "Your joking nobody could be that stupid"

"Oh yes we could" I continued

So off we went and located a trough about eight feet long and carried it to the river. The river was deep but not running fast so we carefully lowered it into the water, it floated perfectly. We grabbed our rods and got on board. Cubby used his rod to launch the boat and I dangled my line behind as we floated away.

"Yes this really was a good idea Cubby"

"I get them sometimes" He grinned.

We had not noticed James approaching and that he had a good view of our antics.

Things went well until we struck a large submerged boulder. There was a cracking noise and the bottom fell out of the 'boat'. We dropped immediately through jamming the frame of the trough under our arms. We were stuck with our legs paddling like hell. We must have looked like a large duck with four legs.

"Stop Bill" Mary interrupted again "Your making me laugh too much and my ribs are sore"

"Well you said to be funny"

"Yes maybe but not that funny this is hilarious"

I continued.

"I agree and so did James as when he arrived we heard him howling with laughter"

"Could you not see the bottom was rotten you daft buggers"

We struggled for what seemed minutes and then thankfully the frame gave way and parted allowing us to swim to the bank side.

That was when we notice our rods floating away. We were surprise to see them followed by a fish jumping.

James who was now laughing uncontrollably shouted.

"You have a fish on the end of your line pity there's no one on the other end. Oh this just gets better and better"

Mary laughed out loud. "I thought it could not get funnier but it certainly has"

I continued again.

At this Cubby took chase.

"I'll catch them at the bridge"

James and I sat on the bank side eating the snack he had brought.

About halve a mile downstream was a crossing point which is what we should have used in the first place.

"I was going to replace that trough when I got time, but we will not tell Cubby, let's make him feel guilty and get him to make a new one"

James was still laughing when Cubby returned holding the rods in his right hand and a large trout in the other.

"A trout for a trough" James smiled.

"Bloody expensive fish that is"

We all sat on the bank eating, Cubby and I soaking wet, but still seeing the humour of the event.

"That's the end of my story so what do you think of me now?"

She smiled at me.

"You know Bill I had heard about your duel and had assumed you were just a typical man thinking that fighting was the solution to everything, but you're not I think there is more to you than that"

I noticed her lean forward and pick something up.

"Look, it's a piece of quartz crystal you do not get that around here the river must have washed it down from the hills"

She handed it to me.

"They make good jewellery you know"

After inspecting this small fragment, I discretely tucked it away. It would be a reminder of her.

"I'm still cold"

Mary snuggled tightly into me and I put my arms around her. Although I was enjoying the moment I hoped Cubby would not be too long as I was getting more concerned about her.

It was not long before I heard a noise and placed my finger on her lips for her to stay quiet. A number of horses rattled over the bridge and stopped.

We waited in anticipation.

"Are you here Bill?" I recognised Cubby's voice immediately.

"Under the bridge" I shouted "I will need a hand to get Mary out"

Her brothers leapt off the bridge to help her.

They had brought a horse and cart with them and spread a bale of hay to form a bed for Mary. They soon got her comfortable and ready to go.

"Bill" she beckoned.

I leant over the cart expecting her thanks. She slapped my hard across the face.

"You know what that's for" She said smiling at me.

I knew I had stared at her bare breasts and guessed that was what she meant. Her smile however compensated for the slap.

Her brother John looked me straight in the eyes.

"This changes nothing; your day of reckoning is still to come but not today"

At this they rode away. Cubby handed me the reigns of my horse and we headed towards Jedburgh but this time by the shortest route.

"I hope this letter wasn't urgent as it will have to wait until tomorrow; we will have to find somewhere to stay tonight and may be have a pint of ale"

"Now you are talking Cubby, this time I will listen to you"

"By the way was that slap worthwhile?"

"That would be telling

Chapter Seven
The Raid

—

Breakfast was usually around day break and all four of us would eat together unless Andrew was away on business. He was quite often away all night and would stay with Walter at Cessford Castle which was not thought unusual as he was Deputy Warden. This morning Andrew sat with us.

"We need to talk after we have finished breakfast so you boys don't rush off"

We hurried our food as he had got our attention.

Andrew spoke quietly.

"I know you boys aren't stupid and have guessed some of my nights away have not been on Deputy Warden's business. Walter and I quite often indulge in old fashioned border business"

We knew immediately what he meant.

"We are currently planning something which you boys can help with; but only if you want"

Cubby responded without waiting for my opinion

"Of course we will help we're family aren't we?"

"Of course you are, but our business is on the English side of the border and Bill might find that difficult"

Andrew looked at me.

"I have no problem so long as my family in Coquetdale are not involved"

I was not fully comfortable but found it impossible to refuse.

"That's good"

"What do you want us to do?" Cubby was enthusiastic.

"Tomorrow night we intend to remove some cattle from the north end of Redesdale and it would help if you could organise a diversion at the southern end"

"How will we do that?" Cubby enquired

"I will give you some oil and rags and if you can fire a barn or just some haystacks that should attract their attention long enough for us carry out our work. There is no moon tonight so we only need two or three hours start"

"That sound easy enough doesn't it Bill?"

"Well at least it's not one of your bright ideas so it has some chance of success"

Andrew continued "But it's not that simple because we need the diversion as soon as it gets dark so you will have to get down Redesdale in daylight without being detected. So yours is a dangerous mission, but you are both young and have two of the best mounts in Scotland, and I would not send you if I thought you could not manage it"

"When will we go?" Cubby was still keen.

"About midday tomorrow should give you time enough"

For the rest of the day all Cubby could talk about was the impending raid. He discussed in detail all the various routes we could take, which ones were rarely used, which ones gave the best cover, which ones were the quickest. None seemed to fulfil all the requirements. He eventually stopped his deliberations.

"What do you think Bill?"

He was finally interested in my opinion.

"I think it would be best to head down Coquetdale as no one would be surprised to see us there. Then cut across the moor heading south of Otterburn. The track there is no good for driving cattle so it is not often used"

Cubby agreed.

"I should have left the planning to you Bill you know that area better than me"

"Yes but a lot of years have passed since I lived in Coquetdale"

Early in the afternoon of the following day we set off following the old Roman road towards the west of Coquetdale. We crossed the Coquet then headed south along a narrow track. We had not expected to meet anyone but as we reached a high point on the track six riders came into view. We could see them clearly so they must also have seen us.

"What should we do?" Cubby was apprehensive.

"Let's just bluff it out" I could see no alternative because if we ran it could ruin the whole plan as we would be heading in the wrong direction.

As they approached I could see they were five men and a boy. All except the boy were fully armed with swords and lances and looked formidable. They reached us and stopped.

"Who are you?" What seemed to be the leader asked.

"I'm Bill Charlton from Haugh Farm and this is my brother Cubby.

"What is your business here?"

"Ours" I replied.

"Don't get funny with us, search them" He commanded.

They grabbed Cubby's saddle bag and tipped it onto the track.

Out fell the rags and a bottle of oil.

"So you intend to partake in some arson do you?"

We were now in trouble unless I could think of something.

"Of course not" I replied still thinking.

"We are crystal collectors heading for caves in the Wannies and we need these for torches"

"Do you think we are stupid?" Their leader was not impressed.

"No, look here" I took the piece of quartz crystal that Mary had found and handed it to him.

"We have a customer for these in Berwick who makes them into jewellery"

I could see he was now almost persuaded. Then I noticed one of the seemed to recognise me. He had fought with us the day I had killed Mark Elliot.

"I know this man; he is who he says he is. I suggest you head to Elsdon and stay in the inn tonight as it would be dark before you reach the Wannies. I would not use the track we have just come along it is boggy and dangerous"

I sensed he was warning me but what about I did not understand.

"Alright get on your way" The leader took command again.

We did not hang around and rode in the direction of Elsdon.

As we passed them I could see that the boy's legs were tied firmly in the stirrups.

We travelled until they were out of sight then turned south towards our intended destination.

"What was that all about?" Cubby asked.

"Did you not see the boy's legs were tied up? I think they had taken a hostage"

Cubby had not noticed but understood the implications.

"So that's why they did not want us to take the same track as them, in case we gave away their route"

From that point onwards we were more careful and did not meet anyone else. We stopped at the edge of a wooded area looking down on a small farm about a quarter of a mile away. The house was a bastle type building with a barn. This would be perfect for our distraction. We took our horses a couple of hundred yards into the woods and tied them securely then found a fallen tree and sat using it as a backrest. Our task would be easy once it was dark.

We sat quietly until nightfall. The farm owner lived in the room on the first floor and when he retired for the night he pulled up the ladder from outside making his house secure against raiders. Once he had done this we prepared to make our move only to be distracted by a large number of riders. They passed by without noticing us.

There must have been at least a hundred. It was a moonless night and obviously more than just the Kerrs were taking advantage of this.

They were heading north of the farmhouse where we had noticed some cattle. We sat quietly until they were a safe distance away.

"We're buggered now" Cubby exclaimed.

"Did you notice they're Armstrongs you cannot mistake Wanless"

"What if they are that doesn't help us"

"Maybe we can make them the diversion" I had an idea

I explained that on top of the bastle house was a beacon which was to be lit in the case of a raid. The Armstrong were by now a good mile away and being expert at their business would not be detected but if we could light the beacon it would really put the cat among the pigeons.

"How will we do that?"

"Well Cubby you have your bow with you and we have oil and rags. If we get close enough you could hit the beacon with a fire arrow"

"I'd have to be really close to do that"

I could see that the area south of the house was a bog and that a drainage ditch ran from just outside the woods past the house feeding into a large pond.

"It's about a hundred yards to the start of the ditch if we crawl to it we can get close to the house undetected"

"And I'm the one that's supposed to get the crazy ideas"

Cubby was smiling as we moved off on our hands and knees.

The ditch was damp and stank the closer you got to the house. It was obviously used for more than just drainage.

We got to the back of the house out of sight of the Armstrongs on the other side. We could see the beacon and knew it would be an iron frame filled with fire wood but it was covered by a sheet of canvas to keep it dry.

"Can you hit it from here?"

"Yes but we had better get two of three arrows prepared in case I don't manage it first time" Cubby seemed confident.

We prepared the arrows and lay them on the side of the ditch.

I lit all three. Cubby fired the first but it must have hit the iron frame and bounced off setting fire to loose hay. The second and third both hit the target. The canvas smouldered then burst into flames. The beacon was now well alight. Within a few minutes a beacon about a mile south of us could be seen.

Everyone in the south of Redesdale was now aware of the raid. The Armstrongs no longer needing to hide their presence were now shouting and firing pistols to chase the cattle away as quickly as possible. They knew that the families of Redesdale would soon be heading their way.

Cubby and I looked at each other as if to agree that this plan had worked perfectly. Then it dawned on us that we were trapped. We had the pond to the west, south was a bog and if we moved back towards the woods the burning hay would make us visible. If we attempted to move, we might get caught and I was sure we would not be able to talk our way out of that. So we had to hide in the ditch until the hay burnt itself out and hoped it would do so before dawn. We were lucky in a couple of hours the hay was just smouldering and we managed to get back to the woods. Although it was still dark we rode towards Coquetdale almost at a full gallop.

We stopped once we felt safe to water the horses in the Coquet. The silence was broken by the sound of someone running. He had not noticed us and almost ran into me. I grabbed him.

"Let me go" He shouted in what was not a man's voice.

I had caught the boy we had seen tied to the horse.

"Who are you?"

"I'm Thomas Armstrong son of John Armstrong"

It turns out he had followed the raiding party only to get lost and to be caught by the five men we encountered. The group knowing who he was were going to hand him over to Sir John Forster who would be overjoyed to have a hostage of such importance.

"How did you get away?"

"I said I needed to pee and they untied me; they did not realise I am a fast runner and I got away in the dark. I hid under a blackberry bush until they moved away"

The poor boy was bleeding all over his hands and face but you had to admire his spirit.

"If you come with us I will see you get back to Scotland and home. We are Kerrs and have no animosity towards the

Armstrongs so you will be safe with us. Put him on your horse Cubby and let's get moving"

"Why on my horse?"

"You're lighter than me"

"That's always your excuse"

"Yes but I can't help that"

We hardly had time to move when we heard riders approaching. Quick Tom you had better hide in the bushes until we find out who they are. As they got closer it was obvious they were the same five riders we had met yesterday. Their leader rode straight up to me leaned over and spoke sarcastically.

"Got lost have you?"

"No" I replied and then fabricated a story.

"We decided not to stop at the inn as we are a bit short of cash. We were camped in some woods in Redesdale when all hell broke out. Beacons were lit and a huge raid was taking place. We just got the hell out of there before anyone saw us"

I could see he had accepted my story.

"Yes it was a major Armstrong raid and I know you are not an Armstrong but that youngster we had caught was one of them who we were going to hand over to the Warden Forster"

I continued with my lying.

"I thought I recognised the lad"

"So you have seen him?"

"Yes" I replied. "About a mile or so back I saw a lad running up the Coquet obviously to hide his tracks. You had better be quick he is a hell of a fast runner"

As he turned to leave he looked back.

"I would appreciate it if you did not mention this in case we do not catch him; Forster would not be happy"

"I will not say a word"

"Thanks, I am sure we will meet again" At this they rode away at speed.

Cubby just looked at me.

"You're the best liar I know I will never believe another word you say"

"Come on Tom we had better get a move on while our luck holds"

It was dawn now so we were able to ride at a full gallop and could no longer be caught. I was pleased when we reached the farm. For what we had expected to be a simple task had turned out to be quite an adventure. Andrew was waiting at the door but before he could speak I had to let him know who we had with us in case he mentioned the raid.

"This is Tom Armstrong; John Armstrong's son we have rescued him from Forster's men"

"Bill" Andrew shook his head. "There are always complications with you, what are you going to do with him"

"I will take him home you never know we might need a favour from the Armstrongs someday"

"That is probably wise Bill. But have some breakfast first while I sort out some fresh horses"

We sat round the table eating and passing pleasantries without mentioning what had taken place the night before. Helen sat down next to Cubby and could not resist placing her hand on top of his. She had obviously been worried but with Tom being there we could not tell her what had happened. Tom was smiling for the first time he knew he was safe and that he would soon be home. His father must fear the worst when his son had not returned from a raid which had been detected.

"Come on Tom we had better go your father will be worried"

As he stood up Cubby rose to join us.

"I'll get the horses Bill"

I noticed Helen's glance.

"You stay Cubby I will only travel in Kerr land until I reach Armstrong territory so there is no danger"

"Are you sure Bill you will be on Ferniehirst land?"

"Of course, I'll be alright they are still in my debt, anyway you have a wife to look after and how can I take all the credit if you are with me?"

Helen grabbed his hand and they both smiled at me knowing I was giving them a chance to spend some time together.

Tom and I mounted our horses and trotted off.

We chatted as we rode.

"How did they catch you?"

"I was not supposed go with them on the raid but I sneaked out and when I tried to catch up I rode into those men who I thought were Armstrongs"

"Don't worry it's an easy mistake to make in the dark"

"You're Bill Kerr aren't you; you killed Jock Campbell in man to man combat"

"Some people call me that"

As I got to know this boy I liked him, he was young but brave. Even when he was captured and tied to the horse I had sensed defiance and he had escaped at the first opportunity.

We travelled for an hour or so alone before encountering a couple of riders. I recognised them from a distance so we had nothing to worry about.

She pulled up next to me smiling.

"Trespassing on our land again do you never learn?"

"Hello Mary you seem to have recovered well"

I was pleased to see her.

"I'm fine, who is that with you"

"It's Tom Armstrong I'm seeing him safely home he has just escaped from Forster's men"

Mary laughed.

"So you are now the protector of both women and children; does he know what you really are?"

"His father does"

She leaned over and put her hand on my arm.

"Be careful, you will be safe on our land won't he Andrew?"

Her brother nodded in agreement, I was pleased it was not John he may not have been so kind.

We smiled at each other then went our separate ways.

"What does she mean by what you really are?"

Tom had picked up her comment.

"She once called me an idiot and probably still thinks that"

I knew she meant did they know I was English which would be dangerous in Armstrong land.

"That's not nice" Tom responded.

"I'm sure she does not mean it and only said it to tease me"

At this point Mary returned and rode alongside me.

"I thought I had better escort you through our land in case you get into trouble"

"Me" I said as if shocked at her insinuation.

"Yes you, you never mean to, but whenever you try to help you always end up in trouble"

"I'll just have to stop helping people then"

"That'll be the day" Mary laughed

We chatted until we reached the boundaries of Ferniehirst land almost to the point of ignoring Tom.

"See you" Mary waved and headed away.

"I think she likes you" Tom commented.

"Get away"

I dismissed Tom's opinion but deep down really hoped he was right.

I turned to watch her ride away only to see her returning as fast as she left.

"I thought so long as I've gone so far I may as well go with you the rest of the way" She smiled and rode on my left with Tom on my other side.

"There I told you" Tom said quietly so Mary would not hear.

"What did he say?" She asked

"Nothing much only that we are nearly there"

I tried to make light of it as maybe we were reading too much into her return.

As we approached Hollows Tower a rider greeted us. It was Wanless.

"You're alive; thank God for that your father is in a foul mood"

As we reached the tower Tom ran upstairs to his father. When we caught up John had his arms around his son. He looked at me.

"Thank you Bill this time you have brought me much more than a share of a ransom"

"I am only responsible for his delivery he escaped from Forster's men all on his own"

"Those English bastards are brave with children we will soon see if they can handle men"

"You are not contemplating armed retaliation?"

I was concerned that I might have stirred up a hornet's nest.

"Of course not, there's no profit in that, we will hit them where it hurts most, in their pockets. All the lands under Forster's jurisdiction will now be our main target whenever we go riding"

He then noticed Mary standing behind me.

"I am sorry we are forgetting our manners. Bill are you not going to introduce your Lady friend?"

"Sorry I thought you knew each other; this is Mary Kerr of Ferniehirst"

"I thought it was but could not understand what she was doing with a Cessford albeit you're just an adopted one"

"It's a long story but she was only making sure I had safe passage through their land"

"Well, as far as I am concerned I know nothing about your intentions regarding Forster so I will be getting on my way"

I headed for the door.

"Wait Bill is there no way I can repay you?"

"No" I replied "I was just being a good neighbour"

"Well I must do the same there is no way you are leaving without a decent meal any way I want to hear the full story about you and Mary"

I could tell that John would be offended at a refusal and anyway I was feeling peckish.

"Come sit down and I will get you some ale"

He gestured at the long table. I sat down with Mary at my side facing John and his son.

"Excuse me for a second I will get my Wife to organise some ale and food then join us "

This she duly did providing us with quite a spread of different meats, bread with just a few vegetables.

We were given what must have been their best silver plates the normal pewter ones being discretely removed.

"Right Mary are you going to tell me how you know this big bugger?"

John was interested.

Mary gave me a push on the shoulder and smiled.

"I'm not sure if he saved my life but at least he saved my father from paying a ransom but I can say it was a painful experience"

"Is this your new business Bill because if it is you're not making any money from it?"

John laughed out aloud.

"Our white knight saves ransoms instead of damsels. Go on Mary tell me the full story"

Mary kindly obliged and described everything just as I had remembered it. John must have been engrossed with the story as he listened intensely without once lifting his tankard of ale.

I spent the whole time just looking at Mary who occasionally glanced my way giving just the hint of a smile.

"So this is the first time you have met since then? That's not a very romantic end to the story"

John had obviously read more into Mary accompanying me on this visit.

I tried to save any embarrassment with.

"I think it would take a lot more than this before any relationship between a Ferniehirst and a Cessford would be tolerated"

"Yes I think Bill is right"

Mary put her hand on my arm.

"But I hope we will always be friends; you never know I may need rescued again"

Mary made light of our situation little knowing the next time we would meet I would come to her aid in much more perilous circumstances.

By now it was turning dark so I made this the excuse for us to take our leave.

"Thanks for the hospitality John but I must get Mary home before her family start to worry"

"They know I can take care myself"

Mary retorted as if offended by my suggestion that I had to look after her.

"Anyway they know I have the great Bill Kerr as my personal body guard"

There was the pretence of sarcasm in her voice but her face gave away her sense of humour.

We shook hands with John and his wife before collecting our horses and heading north.

Although early evening it was a moonless night and the stars seemed to sparkle even more brightly. It could well have been a romantic setting but not for long. Ominously dark clouds quickly covered the sky, a storm was brewing, and the Cheviots was not a place to be caught on such a night.

We could see lightning flashes on the hills ahead of us and as the time between the flash and the noise of the thunder was reducing it was obvious it was heading our way. Crossing these hills on horseback offered a good target so we needed to find a safe shelter. It was raining hard now and our cloaks were soon sodden and provided little protection.

"There's a shepherds shiel down in the valley about a mile away"

Mary shouted through the rain with confidence

"I'm pleased you know the area, you lead and I will follow, and we had better hurry"

We galloped as fast as the rain and conditions would allow. We reached the building leapt from our horses, tied them up quickly and rushed inside. It was a small building only about three paces along each dimension.

On one wall was a small fireplace, on the adjacent wall there was a raised planked area which the shepherd could use either as a seat or bed. Luckily we found a lantern which still contained some oil and using a store of dry chopped wood that was stacked in one corner we soon made ourselves comfortable. In was a handy little building which the shepherd would use only occasionally when it was not worthwhile travelling home if he would be coming back next day.

Because of this it lacked many homely comforts.

"You had better take off some of those wet clothes"

I suggested removing my drenched cloak.

"I'm surprised you have not suggested we take off our clothes and huddle to keep warm; if that ever crossed your mind you can forget it"

She was right but I did not admit to it.

"No I only meant our outer garments we can dry out the rest sitting in front of the fire"

I pulled out the platform so we could both sit on it facing the fire which was by now well ablaze.

Mary suddenly burst out laughing.

"Bill why is it every time we meet it ends up in disaster"

"Must be fate" I replied

"At least there are no broken bones"

"Not yet" Mary was still laughing.

"It's a good job the shepherd had the forethought to leave a lantern and firewood"

"It's one of ours and we like our shepherds to keep these buildings in a usable condition. I'll mention it when I get home so the shepherd can bring more oil the next time he comes"

For a moment I had forgotten how extensive the Ferniehirst estate was and the importance of Mary's family. Compared to me she was almost royalty yet here we were in the same predicament and able to see the humour of it.

"Last time Mary we spent only an hour or so wet and cold hiding under that bridge. This time I think it will be a few hours before this storm subsides"

I tried to start a conversation.

"All I can remember was the pain, I may have been wet and cold but I can't recall that. I know you kept me talking so I would not fall asleep. So sitting in front of a nice warm fire is not too bad no matter what the weather is like outside"

She bent forward and threw another log on the fire.

We could see the lightning through a small piece of dirty glass that acted as a window.

"I think the lightning has stopped"

I was hinting that maybe we could make a move.

"But it's still raining so we may as well wait till first light and hopefully it may have stopped by then. Anyway it's dark and slippery and I don't want my horse to fall again"

I was pleased with her decision. We sat and talked all night. I recalled some of my pranks with Cubby which she found hilarious especially our messing with the bull "Samson" and when we stole the pig.

"You must have had a great time when you lived in the farm with James"

"They were the best times of my life"

With the thought of it I felt a tear forming. Before I could turn away she wiped it with her hand.

"I've said it before you may be a great warrior but deep down you're a big softie"

She stood up.

"Come on let's move this so we can both lean against the wall and maybe manage a nap"

We tried to get some sleep well at least she did as she lay back with her eyes closed. I could not help but sit and look at her. She kept smiling although she could not see I guess she sensed it.

My thoughts turned to the old woman's prophecy. I had a new home, family and had even used a new name, as predicted, but was she right in love as well. I then recalled the time I saw Mary and shielded my eyes from the sunlight was this what she meant by the light would show me the way. I certainly hoped it was.

When morning came there were almost no clouds in the sky. I felt sorry for the poor horses that had spent the night without shelter but they seemed no worse for it. Our cloaks were still damp but warm so we put them on and headed north again.

The air was clear and the hills filled with that fresh smell you get after the rain. Mary and I talked very little as we were both tired. We made steady progress without pushing the horses. Soon we could see Ferniehirst castle.

"You had better leave me now so I won't have any explaining to do"

I agreed and stopped my horse but waited until she was safely inside the castle then headed for home.

On my way I wondered if fate had taken a hand in this I definitely hoped this was the case.

Chapter Eight
The Reprisal

O n frequent occasions Cubby and I would head back to Coquetdale and visit the farms to see how Esther and Ella were managing. She had spent my money wisely, the farm was now in good repair, and she had even managed to buy more cattle. I was happy that they were now self-sufficient so I did not interfere in case they thought I was checking up on them. We would visit only long enough to exchange pleasantries then head off to the inn at Alwinton.

We were always made welcome and in fact had become friendly with Harry who everyone referred to as Nebby. He was good company and gave us shelter in his small cottage on the outskirts of the village. On one of our visits he was unusually quiet which did not hamper his drinking but suggested he had something on his mind.

"You know Bill I could not give a bugger about Kings and Queens, whether you are English or Scottish, in the borders its family that counts"

"I agree" I replied without understanding where the comment had come from.

"I need to tell you something" He leant over, put his hand on my shoulder, and continued quietly.

"Forster is planning a reprisal raid; he is fed up with your warden not handing over Armstrongs and Kerrs. He knows the recent raids in Redesdale were two separate raids one by the Armstrongs and the other further North by the Kerrs so he has decided to cross the border and seek justice himself"

"How did he find out Kerrs were involved?"

He had got my attention.

"Forster has paid informers on both sides of the border who frequent the ale houses to pick up information, I am sure the Kerrs do the same"

"When will Forster make his move?" I questioned

"Don't know but it will be in the next few days as he is calling a muster and as you know we are obliged to take part"

"This will be a major raid then" I was becoming concerned

"I guess at least 3,000 riders; I know the Armstrongs and Kerrs can muster more than that given sufficient time"

He was right this raid was not expected.

"Look here" Nebby continued

"The Robson family and their associates will be wearing red armbands on their sword arms"

At this he took out a piece of red material and tore off two strips giving one to each of us.

"If there is any chance of us meeting in conflict wear these"

I gratefully accepted them.

"Thanks I will not divulge where we obtained this information; we need to leave as soon as possible but not too early so as to draw attention to ourselves. We will then head off in the direction of your cottage so no one will be the wiser"

I smiled.

"Got time for a couple of more Ale though, whose round is it?"

"Must be mine" Nebby replied "Obviously that information had no value"

"Oh, all right then Cubby will buy them, the Kerrs are his family"

Cubby reluctantly agreed but commented.

"So you're only a Kerr when it suites you"

We had a few more drinks and left the inn fairly early but not too early as to be suspicious.

We reached the cottage and I shook Nebby by the hand.

"You're right in the end its family that matters"

We rode off into the night

We arrived home in the early hours and agreed to get some sleep and leave the discussion with Andrew until the morning.

Cubby got Helen to make an early breakfast so we could talk things over with Andrew.

"Are we absolutely positive this will happen?" Andrew was concerned that we did not cry wolf.

"There is no doubt we have been informed by someone who will be involved"

"Damn" Andrew cursed "I knew something like this would happen; James Stewart and his Lords of the Congregation have been so busy fighting with Mary of Guise that the borders have been out of control. Thankfully she died recently and James Stewart has control of Parliament"

"You talk as if you know him" I enquired.

"Yes he is a Protestant and although we Kerrs are Catholic we don't like the French and he has kicked them out of Scotland so we are grateful for that"

"Will he help us" Cubby asked.

"Probably, he owes me a favour; we fought together about ten years ago when we ejected an English force out of Fife. He was a Catholic priest turned Protestant, allied with the English, and with their help over through Mary of Guise. He is very ambitious and will see this as an opportunity to strengthen his position"

Andrew continued.

"Do we know which route they will be taking?"

"No not yet. They are to seek out Armstrongs and Kerrs, who are blamed for numerous thefts of cattle, so that limits their options. I was told that they are to muster at Chow Green, at the end of Coquetdale, where the old Roman ruins are"

Andrew thought for a while.

"They could go North or South from there but I doubt that they will start with Cessford Castle as only Edinburgh and Stirling are stronger. I guess they will head down Liddlesdale and then up the Esk where most of the Armstrongs live before heading towards Jedburgh and Ferniehirst Castle. Hopefully the Armstrongs will slow them down enough for us to make preparations"

"Is there anything Bill and I can do?" Cubby was offering our services.

"At this stage there are three things to do; seek assistance from Lord James Stewart in Edinburgh, muster as many as we can from our family and associates, and finally track all Forster's movements"

He paused.

"We need to split our resources otherwise we may be too late. Cubby you are by far our best rider and have a superb horse so can you head down Liddlesdale and keep an eye out? I will contact Walter at Cessford Castle and gather our forces, Bill you will have to go to Edinburgh and warn James Stewart"

"I don't mind that, but will he receive me?"

"Yes you have my son's sword and here" He passed me his ring.

"James Stewart gave me this ring and he has seen the sword which he knows I had specially made for my son. Announce yourself as Bill Kerr son of Andrew Kerr of Cessford and I guarantee he will receive you"

"Helen, pack some food for Cubby and Bill I will get on my way"

He turned back as he left.

"Be careful Cubby you have the more dangerous task, we will all meet at Jedburgh in four days"

Our duties were clear.

Helen hugged Cubby before we mounted, and I shook his hand prior to proceeding in opposite directions. I can't remember shaking his hand before, usually it was a pat on the back or some wise crack as we parted. But it seemed the right thing to do as confirmation that this was no game we were playing.

Edinburgh was a day and a half ride the most difficult part being the Cheviot Hills after which the going was fairly easy. Thankfully, although it was early autumn, the track was dry. I rode until darkness made it dangerous. It was not a journey I had made before so I had to be more careful than usual. I tried to sleep under a large oak tree in case it rained but it was a clear night and I lay admiring the stars. I was probably nervous about the next day but would have denied this at the time. At daybreak I headed off.

About mid-morning I knew I was approaching Edinburgh as the smell was overpowering. I had been warned that I would smell it before I could see it. I eventually could see the Castle perched on the rocky outcrop. This was not my destination I had to head east of the castle for about a mile to reach Holyrod

Palace. It was a magnificent building, new and very ornate. I was met by guards before huge wooden doors.

"I am Bill Kerr son of Andrew Kerr of Cessford seeking an audience with Lord James Stewart"

I expected a positive response but got.

"Bugger off we have not seen you before"

"Here" I handed over the ring

"Show him this and he will see me"

I was made to wait standing outside as they were obviously sure I was of no consequence.

Eventually a guard returned.

"He will see you, come this way"

I was led through a long hall and into a narrow room. At the end of the room sat who I assumed was James Stewart. He was a slim man with sharp features and a pointed beard.

"Hand me his sword and dirk then leave us"

They were both passed to him.

"Come here and sit"

I sat on a chair facing him.

"I remember this sword your father had made for you. See here as you pull it from the scabbard you see the sun rising. Andrew and I had joked that hopefully it would be the last sunrise an enemy would see"

"But you are not Bill Kerr, you see the sun emblem is only on one side of the blade and as you would draw it this would point towards you and not the enemy, to see it you have to be left handed as are most of the Kerrs"

"Maybe not but I am by action and fate"

"Fate; that interests me tell me your story, I know Andrew must trust you otherwise he would not have given you the sword and ring"

I told him my story which he listened to with interest.

"Here" He handed the ring back

"I gave this to Andrew for saving my life, that is when he got that scar, but I bet he didn't tell you that, and you did not tell me it was you who killed Jock Campbell in man to man combat. You may not be his son but you have his modesty. Why have you come?"

I explained that John Forster was preparing to raid Scotland and was targeting Armstrongs and Kerrs and we needed his help to stop him.

"Help the Armstrongs? My father tricked their leader the old Johnnie Armstrong and hung him and about thirty of his party and this still rankles with them. I do however object to this raid into my country, but I have to be careful as I suspect there are politics involved"

He went on to explain.

"I and the Protestant Lords of the Congregation have taken over from the Catholic Mary of Guise but there is still animosity between some of the Scottish clans. Our Queen Mary is married to the Dauphin of France where she resides. Elizabeth believes we are at our weakest at the moment and she is probably right. So if our response to this raid is not controlled or if we pursue them into England this could give an excuse for an invasion. I must however take some action otherwise it will be seen as weakness. You are sure this raid will take place?"

"Yes, some of my relatives in England are involved"

"I will give you 300 lancers under the command of Captain Murray and these are available immediately. I will raise a much larger force and meet in Jedburgh a couple of days later. Hopefully the matter will have been resolved by then"

He escorted me to the door and instructed one of the guards to fetch the Captain at once.

"Get your horse and wait outside the main entrance Murray will meet you there. It has been interesting to meet you Bill Kerr I think you had better continue using that name"

We shook hands and I left to collect my horse.

Within an hour Murray arrived with his lancers.

"So you're the famous Bill Kerr. Jock Campbell was a real bastard he once provoked one of my men into a fight and killed him, so you are among friends."

"I am told we have to head for Jedburgh and meet up with riders from your family before deciding upon what action we must take"

"That's right by the time we get there we should have a good idea of what is happening"

I liked Murray and could tell he had the respect of his men. I sensed they were used to action

After an overnight camp we moved into Jedburgh and gathered outside the ruined Abbey. About mid-afternoon Walter and Andrew arrived with about 300 riders soon to be followed by John Ferniehirst and another 200 riders.

We gathered the leaders together to see what intelligence we had if any. No one had any news and I was beginning to worry if I had been duped. John was first to comment.

"I have no definite news other than Mary had gone to one of the outlying farms to help a wife who was in labour and had not returned"

"Where is Cubby?"

I hoped he was alright.

Andrew replied "We haven't heard anything yet, but I am sure he is alright"

No sooner had he said this than a rider arrived at full gallop. It was Cubby. He dismounted and joined us.

"What's the situation?" Andrew enquired.

"About two days ago Forster and a force of about 3000 raided the farms of the Armstrongs and surrounded Hollows Tower.

They captured about a dozen Armstrongs and when John refused to give up the tower they drowned six of them in the Esk. I doubt they will kill any others otherwise they will have no one to ransom. I managed to warn most of our families but could not reach all of them. The force has now split into two about half still surrounding Hollows Tower and holding Armstrongs captive. The other half is camped at Rigg farm and has taken a number of Kerrs as hostages but thankfully none have been killed, at least not yet."

"What about Mary?"

John enquired.

"She is one of the hostages with three couples and a baby. They are being held in an old farm building with guards posted."

"We have to rescue her"

Her brother was clearly concerned.

"That will be very difficult they are well located with good visibility. Any riders will be seen a good ten minutes before they get there. This would place the hostages in real danger. They are also surrounded on three sides by the river and have guards posted so a night rescue is not advisable."

"Could we get close undetected?" I asked

"If we leave now it would be dark before we get there so we could hide behind the hill south of the river."

"In the morning you say it would take ten minutes from first being seen before you reach their camp so we need to find some way of protecting the hostages for that time"

"What's the building like? Could two good men hold the door for the ten minutes needed?" I was hatching a plan.

"Yes if they could get there undetected and overpower the two guards without attracting attention, but that is a lot of ifs"

"Then that has to be our plan I will need someone to go with me"

John volunteered without hesitation.

"She is my sister I will go with you, anyhow I need to see if you are as good as they say you are"

I was happy to use him as he would be fighting to protect his family as there is no greater incentive than that. My reason for going was obvious to Cubby but maybe not to anyone else.

"Bill unless you are extremely lucky this plan is suicidal"

"I have had a charmed life so far and this feels like fate"

We discussed the plan in detail. Cubby advised that we were too many to successfully hide north of the camp and some would have to hide to the east and west. They would take longer than ten minutes to get to the camp.

"That's probably alright as they outnumber us two to one we will have maximum impact if we all appear at once. They are not soldiers and are unlikely to risk their lives for a few hostages. They will not be expecting us this soon as they are unaware we had advance notice"

We agreed to split into three groups the Ferniehirst and Cessford Kerrs would form two and attack from the east and west, Murray and his lancers would charge from the north as they would probably be the quickest.

The plan was complete. Cubby led us away, without him we would have no chance of success. I was really proud of my brother.

Cubby was right as we were all in place about three hours before day break. John and I would now have the dangerous task of reaching the hostages undetected.

We listened carefully to Cubby's advice.

"Although there is no river to the south they have it well guarded so you will have to cross the river. Unfortunately, there is more cover if you reach the river from the north but the building is to the south of the camp. This means you will need to swim about two hundred yards"

I asked if this was the only way as although it was late summer the water was still very cold and two hundred yards was a long way.

Cubby confirmed there was no other way.

"Well at least you will be swimming with the current"

John and I considered the plan. Neither of us were strong swimmers and we needed to have our swords and jacks. That was when Cubby got one of his bright ideas.

"You know those pig skins that we carry the water in if you empty one and blow it up you will be able to strap your sword and jacket to it and use it as a float"

It sounded a good idea but I still remembered the incident with the cattle trough it sounded a good idea as well. But lacking any other suggestions it was worth a try.

We wasted no time and acquired two pig skins, strapped our swords, jacks and boots to them and headed for the river. We crept up to the water's edge and slipped quietly in. It was freezing and I almost shouted out with the shock. As we progressed I noticed two guards talking not far away so we held onto our pig skins and floated with the current. So far so good I thought. That was when I realised that watertight and airtight were not quite the same. Our floats were slowly deflating. After one hundred yards or so they were useless but luckily for us the water from this point was only chest deep. We held our gear above our heads to keep our jacks and boots dry and slowly and quietly reached the rear of three old buildings. There was a small copse of trees behind one of them where we could hide and put on our boots and jacks. We were shivering in the cold night air but thankful that we had completed the part of our task that neither of us had looked forward to.

"I wonder if this is the right building." Ferniehirst whispered.

Our answer came immediately as we heard the cries of a baby.

"That's good, should we take out the guards"

John was keen to see his sister.

"No" I replied "We do not know if they will change the guards before day break and that could give the game away"

There were still a couple of hours before dawn so we just had to wait. After about an hour we could hear two men approaching.

"We have been sent to relieve you"

I heard one of them say.

"We will wait ten minutes then take their place; there should be no further changes"

I looked at Ferniehirst and he nodded.

We picked up a couple of sturdy branches to use as clubs and sneaked each side of the building. We sprang out clubbing the two guards senseless. John and I dragged them into the building. Mary shouted out.

"It's you John"

He put his finger over his mouth to hush her. We then cut the hostages free. We were not surprised to find them roped together as the building was quite dilapidated and therefore not very secure. He then passed the guards swords to two of the freed men.

"Tie them up and gag them, if you have any trouble use the swords"

"Are you staying in here with us?" Mary questioned.

"No Bill and I have to take the guards place otherwise they would be missed, but don't worry help will arrive in the morning"

So we stood outside as if on guard. I was concerned that we were both big men as one of the guards was fairly short.

Thankfully no one noticed.

As dawn was breaking we kept looking towards the hill in anticipation hoping they would come before we were noticed.

We did not wait long. The hills around rang out with the sound of horns and all around a great hoard appeared. They looked like thousands. A large proportion of Forster's men did not stop to count them but took to their horses immediately and galloped south. Someone who seemed in command shouted at us.

"Kill the hostages"

We did not move and he realised who we were. He then pointed to a group of four men.

"Kill them and the hostages"

A tall man standing in the shadow of a tree questioned

"What's the profit in that?"

The voice seemed familiar but I could not place it.

"None" their leader replied.

"But they're Kerrs and if they recognise us they will not rest till every one of us is dead"

At this they all charged towards us but John and I stood firm just inside the doorway. He stood to my left and was another left handed Kerr so we could both swing our swords freely. Only two at a time could get at us so we were able to fend them off. Our two attackers once wounded retreated only to be replaced by the other two. Their commander could see we were holding our ground and ordered another two to get lances and help. Now we were in trouble. As they charged forward I heard a dull thud and one fell to the ground with an arrow in his chest. It was Cubby firing from the copse. The other managed to get his lance over one of the attackers and plunge it into Ferniehirsts shoulder breaking his collar bone. He dropped his sword grabbed the lance and pulled the assailant forward. As he fell over his comrade and I cracked his scull with my sword. It was now two against one and I really was in trouble. It was then that Mary charged screaming swinging her brother's sword. She was like a wild cat with her red hair flying. At this our opponents made a hasty retreat. But before I could catch my breath another two were ordered forward. They charged with swords held high and I noticed the red band. As our swords clashed I shouted.

"Harry it's me, Bill"

"You daft bugger, where's your armband" he turned to his pal.

"They're family Tom so we had better make this look good"

"Sorry Harry but I must have lost it in the river"

I then pleaded.

"Don't make this too strenuous I'm just about buggered"

An exhibition of swordplay then took place for the benefit of anyone watching; luckily Cubby had noticed the armbands and kept out of it.

As Murray's men approached the rest of Forster's men took to their horses so Harry and his pal joined them. Harry turned as he left and smiled.

"Good job you noticed my armband or I would have killed you for sure"

I laughed "Of course you would"

Their leader passed us covering his face with his helmet. He obviously feared the Kerr family with good reason as I would find out later. His subterfuge was unsuccessful as I had recognised him before he realised we had taken the guards place.

All of Forster's men disappeared before our force could reach them. All that were left were the two guards tied up, one lying with an arrow in his chest, and the man whose scull I had cracked.

Murray rode up and dismounted.

"What's next?"

I winked at him.

"James Stewart has 5,000 men at Jedburgh who are on their way now; we are to relieve John Armstrong at Hollows Tower tomorrow"

"That's good we may as well camp here till they arrive"

Cubby then asked.

"What about these two guards"

"Give them their horses and let them go they are not worth ransoming"

They were set free and left at a full gallop.

"Did they hear?"

"Yes Bill they certainly took notice" Mary confirmed

"Good as soon as Forster hears he will return to England probably taking the Armstrong hostages with him. That will leave the Armstrongs with the problem of raising the ransom.

They are no great friends of ours and it serves them right as their excessive reiving gave Forster his excuse"

"So that's it" Murray asked

"Yes you had better send a messenger to Edinburgh before James Stewart has a wasted journey, but stay with your men for a couple of days in Jedburgh just in case there are further developments"

"My men will enjoy that, I am sure we will meet again Bill Kerr"

At this they lined up and rode off two a breast. I wondered if Murray knew who I really was.

"How is John?" I asked Mary

"Sore, I managed to stop the bleeding but I think he is suffering more from broken pride than bones"

She got hold of John under his good arm.

"Bill, give me a hand to get him on his horse"

This I duly obliged and as I did so she leant over, put her hand on my shoulder and whispered.

"Thanks you really are my knight in shining armour"

They rode off together.

Cubby came towards me smiling.

"No slap this time the ungrateful bitch"

I could not help laughing.

"So you were lucky again Eh?"

"With a brother like you I don't need luck, thanks for following me"

"That water was bloody cold wasn't it"

"Too true what we need now is something to warm us up"

"They say that ale can do that"

"Do they? Sounds like another good idea of yours Cubby"

What a day it had been. Over two thousand men involved yet only two fatalities and those at the hands of Cubby and I. I knew it must have been fate.

Chapter Nine
A Traitor Trapped

I found it difficult to settle down after the excitement. Andrew was so proud of us he called us "his boys" every time he talked about us. Helen seemed even more in love with Cubby and the whole house was a happier place. I could not get Mary out of my mind but there was little I could do about it as the relationship between the Ferniehirst and Cessfords had improved very little despite our part in the rescue. I resigned myself to the situation but secretly hoped fate would take a hand. Then one day I thought it had.

I was in the field when I saw a rider approaching leading another horse behind. I could see from the long red hair it was Mary. I leapt onto my horse and galloped towards her. I pulled up alongside her.

"Hello Bill" she smiled at me

"This is for you" and she handed me the reigns.

"You needn't have done this" I was reluctant to accept her gift.

"Oh, it's not from me it's from John, he takes it badly being beholding to a Cessford, it's a matter of pride"

"In that case I will take it, it's a magnificent animal, come I'm sure Helen can fix us something to eat"

"Alright but I can't stay long"

Helen was overjoyed at having another woman in the house despite it being a short stay. She eventually left us alone to prepare some food.

"You know I have never thanked you properly, you have twice saved me from being raped or even murdered"

"I could not let that happen to you" At the thought of it I felt a tear forming and turned to hide it.

She brushed it away with her hand.

"As I have already said for a tough warrior you're just a big softy at heart, and I like you for that"

Helen returned with some cold sliced beef and fresh bread.

The two women talked like old friends and I just sat looking at Mary and smiled every time we exchanged glances.

After half an hour Mary left and I rode part of the way with her.

At supper Helen teased me.

"I liked Mary she is very pretty or had you not noticed?"

"Of course he has, I think he is in love" Cubby joined in the teasing. I slept well that night fate seemed to be clearly on my side.

For the next few days I could hardly do my work for thinking about Mary. Cubby teased me relentlessly. Then one night during supper he was recounting that fateful morning when I mentioned.

"You know I recognised that rider who was shouting out the orders to kill us. It was Walter Dodds the man who had taken ill the night my father was killed"

I noticed a reaction from Andrew.

I looked him straight in the eye and he could tell I had guessed what must have happened.

"The bastard" Andrew called out thumping the table.

"I pay him good money to be our informant and not only does he not tell us about the raid he takes an active part against us"

It made sense now, no wonder he was scared someone in the Kerr family recognised him.

Cubby spurted out "Bill I didn't know this honest. I was told the information came from an overheard conversation at the inn"

Andrew interrupted. "That's right that was the story we put out to protect our source"

I could now understand what had transpired but was still at a loss as to why the encounter had been so deadly and why no attempt was made to take captives for ransom.

I had to question this. "Andrew, why did you think it was necessary to kill everyone?"

I could sense Andrew was uneasy and that his answer in some ways was an attempt to close the whole issue.

"I'm sorry Bill it would appear that we may have acted on false information. One of our neighbours had been killed in a raid and his wife brutally raped. We had been informed by Dodds that the four youths in your party were responsible so our actions were more in revenge rather than just foiling a raid. Now we know he is a traitor and maybe a liar as well it is probable he would have accused anyone for money"

He paused "I think we need to get someone to visit him some night and make sure he does not see morning"

"Don't do that it will be seen as a murder for no good reason and could provoke a response. What we need to do is get him to reveal himself"

"You're probably right Bill but how can we do that?"

"Greed, good old fashioned greed nearly always works"

I thought for a moment.

"You know we have been considering buying a new bull to improve our stock. A good bull is expensive and we would pay good money to know the location of such a bull especially if we could also be told when it would be unguarded"

"That's a good idea Bill, Walter will not be able to resist that. I will make sure our request reaches him through the usual channels "

Andrew smiled.

"What do you intend next?"

"Let's get the bull first, but make sure Walter comes to collect his money after we have the bull"

Andrew gave me a friendly push

"You're a clever bugger"

"No I'm not it is the way James taught me in a fight you can use sword, hands, feet, knees, elbows or anything else if you want to win. But sometimes you can win without even fighting if you use your brains"

We finished supper and all retired.

That night my mind was racing. I had always wondered how easily we had fallen into the ambush. Even if they had known the raid was to take place for them to guess the exact route was either good luck or fate. It turns out it was neither they had been told precisely where we were heading. But then again maybe it was still fate as because of it I met Cubby and his family and now Mary. All this conjecture tired me out and I fell soundly asleep.

It was about four days later Andrew came in from the fields waving a piece of linen cloth.

"Got him"

He almost shouted it out and spread the cloth on the table. It was a map which I looked at carefully.

"That's George Robson's farm. He's almost a relative of mine"

"Is it really?" Andrew laughed

"Don't worry he will get the bull back eventually. I've been told he is off to Berwick market on Wednesday and is not expected back until morning. We should be able to borrow it for a few days. Do you think you and Cubby could manage to collect the animal without being caught?"

"No problem" Cubby was quick to respond

"There are two of us and it is only one animal"

That's when I knew there would be problems whenever Cubby thinks things will be simple they never are.

Wednesday soon came and we travelled into Coquetdale just as it was getting dark. I knew exactly were the farm was so we were soon within a hundred yards or so. We tied our horses to a tree. I carried a strong rope we had brought for the occasion. We proceeded to look for the bull which we soon found.

It was being kept in a small paddock next to the farmhouse. We could see it easily as it was lit up by the light shining from the window.

Obviously George's family were still at home so we would have to be quiet. Moving the bull was not much of a problem but opening the gate was. Its hinges were rusted away and it was secured by two loops of rope tying it to the post. The other end being held by two sturdy branches crossed over the gate. As there were two of us we could manage physically but to do it without making any noise would be difficult.

Cubby and I whispered our plans to each other. He would climb over the gate and hold it steady whilst I removed the outside branch, then I would support it while he removed the other branch. It was just as well we had planned this as when I removed the branch the gate began to give way. Cubby only just held on long enough for me to get back to prevent it crashing down.

It was not so heavy once Cubby removed the other branch but as it had no hinges it was firmly stuck in the mud. Between us we had to lift the gate with pure force and swing it open. It creaked but thankfully not sufficient enough to be detected. Stage one was completed now we only had to lead the bull away.

Thankfully the bull was placid and once Cubby tied the rope around his neck it walked quietly away with us. We got to our horses and Cubby tied the rope to his saddle and we slowly headed for home.

"There, told you it would be easy"

Said Cubby smugly.

"Certainly makes a change"

I could not believe how successful we had been.

"We should be able to move a bit quicker than this now we are out of earshot"

Cubby then yanked on the rope as the bull was lagging behind.

Then it all went wrong. The bull seemed to object and charged away. Cubby turned his horse to restrain the animal to no avail. It removed both saddle and Cubby from the horse giving Cubby an uncomfortable ride for about fifty yards. Then he dug in his heals to try and slow the animal down. This resulted in him being somersaulted into the air landing with a thump on his rear end. It then left Cubby lying in the dirt and disappeared into the darkness.

I should have ridden after the bull then come back for Cubby later. But any sense that I might have deserted me for the moment and I burst out with uncontrollable laughter.

"Thought that was funny?"

A rather annoyed Cubby retorted.

"Absolutely"

Cubby dusted himself off.

"What a ride, I think my arse must be black and blue"

Still laughing I replied "And you will have to ride bare back now"

Cubby smiled, he had calmed down and could now see the funny side.

Although it was dark a bull dragging a saddle was not too difficult a trail to follow. Luckily it had headed in a direction not too far from our intended route so we hoped to catch it before it got its bearings and headed back to the farm.

We eventually followed it into a small wood at the end of the valley. Here our luck had turned. The saddle had become jammed between two trees restraining the bull which by now had settled down.

Cubby collected the saddle and tied the rope to the tree while he saddled the horse.

"It seemed happy enough to be led by hand so maybe I had better do that, anyway I am finding riding a bit uncomfortable at the moment"

"Why is that?" I enquired.

"Just shut up and let's get on our way"

As we slowly headed for home I kept on laughing each time I recalled the spectacle which was quite often. Cubby gave me a dirty look each time but said nothing.

As had been prearranged we left the bull in the paddock that was on James's farm. Although the buildings had been destroyed it was still intact and it was the nearest place.

Cubby managed to ride the rest of the way and we got home just before dawn.

Andrew was waiting for us. "Your late, have any problems?"

Cubby replied firmly. "None at all, we just took our time to be careful"

As he walked away Andrew couldn't help but notice the way he was walking

Andrew looked at me smiling "That's good as I need you to ride to Walter's tomorrow with a message"

Cubby rubbing his behind replied

"No problem"

Cubby doing something without a problem, that'll be a first.

It was only a day later that Andrew met Walter Dodds. As arranged they met at James's farm in clear view of the acquired bull. Andrew handed over five shillings the usual fee he paid for information.

The first part of my plan was now complete. We had the evidence to prove Walter Dodds was quite happy to sell out his neighbours to us across the border but would he now betray us. For the right price we knew he would.

For the second part of my plan I needed George Robson's help so this required a discrete visit. We would visit my Aunt Esther next morning but pay our regards to George as well. He was more than pleased to see us.

"Come on in Bill I've just finished a batch of Ale it's one of my best so you must sample it"

"That's a good idea"

Cubby was quick to take up the offer.

We sat down and chatted for a while before I broached the subject.

"Hear you have lost a bull"

"Yes I have, the only night I have been away in the last month and the bugger was stolen"

"Hell of a coincident then wasn't it?"

"Yes it's as if they knew"

"Well maybe they did"

I waited for a reaction to my comment.

"Do you know something about it"

"All I will say is that one of your drinking pals at the inn was involved"

This got Georges attention.

"Bill do you know who he is"

"Maybe" I replied

"But we need to get some proof"

"What do you suggest Bill, I can tell you have got a plan"

"Simple" I explained

"This weekend when you are in the inn let it be known that you will give two pounds to anyone who may know the whereabouts of your bull or may know of anyone who has just acquired a new bull"

I knew Dodds being a single man who liked a drink was in the inn every weekend. I also now knew how he funded his habit.

"Good idea Bill but I haven't got two pounds and anyway isn't that too much as you could buy a good cow in calf for that"

"Don't worry about that I will lend it to you. Yes, it's a lot but still cheap for a good bull and we need to make it too good for him to turn it down. I will get It back almost immediately" It was now all agreed

"Thanks Bill but there is no need to rush away we may as well enjoy this ale while it's at its best"

That we did with the result we never got to visit Aunt Esther and I don't think George did much work that day.

We left the next stage of our plan in the capable hands of George.

We eventually got to know what transpired that weekend. George waited until everyone had sufficient to drink to remove any inhibitions but still remain competent.

"Listen lads, I know some of you are aware I have lost a bull if you know of anyone over the border who has just received a new bull let me know. If it turns out to be mine there is a two-pound reward for this information"

It did not take long for the bait to be swallowed.

Walter Dodds eventually made his way across the room and sat next to George.

"George, as you know I often trade across the border and always keep my ear to the ground. I have heard of a new bull at a farm this side of Morebattle"

George responded.

"Good that's not too far away so it could well be mine"

"Give me your handkerchief"

George gestured to his brother Percy

"Here Walter there's a piece of charcoal draw me a map. If it is my bull, there will be two pounds for you next week end"

Walter duly obliged with.

"I can't be absolutely sure, but my source is usually reliable"

The second stage of my plan was now complete. Next weekend would now be interesting.

Next day Cubby and I took our fishing rods and sat by the river like we used to do. We sat near the point where we had tried to cross in the trough. This time we actually caught three trout.

We knew George would eventually come. He arrived about mid-day with his brother Percy. They dismounted and walked to us. We all shook hands.

"That is my bull"

"Well it's not ours someone has left him here. We have no idea how he got there have we Cubby?"

Cubby just shook his head.

"Here George take this"

I passed over forty shillings in coins wrapped up in the piece of linen Dodds had given us showing George's farm.

"Are you sure?"

George accepted the money.

"I have only lent it to you I am sure I will get it back at the weekend. Sorry we cannot return your hospitality as you see the buildings are burnt out"

"Don't worry about that you can buy me a pint on Saturday night. That's if you can manage to get to Alwinton"

Cubby replied immediately. "We'll be there. I'm sure it will be an interesting night"

At this they headed on their way. Cubby and I remained for another hour or so as the fishing was good. But I only managed to catch one more.

"That's a big one" Cubby said admiringly as I removed the fish from the hook.

"I think we will hook a bigger one this weekend"

"Yes but what will we do with that catch?"

I had not though about that.

"I would like to gut him like a fish but maybe we can think of something subtler"

We picked up our fish and headed home. We had a good supper that night and never even mentioned Walter Dodds.

Saturday came soon enough. Andrew gave us extra money and sent us on our way with.

"Don't do anything stupid"

"Us" Cubby replied

Andrew shook his head and headed for the door.

"See you in the morning"

We arrived at the inn fairly early as we did not want to miss anything. George and Percy also came early.

I had a quite word with George who passed on some instructions to his brother. We then sat in the corner of the room with our backs to the door. We did not have to wait long before Dodds entered. I heard

"Evening George"

I recognised the voice but did not turn around. I did notice Percy making a discreet exit.

"Here have a seat Walter I have something for you"

"So it was your bull then"

Walter sat down in expectation.

"Yes, so here you are"

George threw the money on the table still raped in the piece of linen. The two pounds made up of forty shillings landed with a thud.

"Thanks very much obviously my source was right"

"I'm not surprised" George went on to say

"You had better give me back Percy's handkerchief before he complains"

Walter unfolded the cloth spilling the coins onto the table and then for some reason held it up by the corners in a humorous gesture suggesting it was dirty. That was when his smile disappeared he was not holding up a handkerchief he was holding up the map of Georges farm for all to see.

Before he could move Cubby grabbed his arm and I removed his sword.

"I was only selling information, no one got hurt"

"Not this time but lives have been lost in the past through your treachery"

I pointed his sword at his gullet.

"Maybe I should slit your throat"

I had not notice Reverent Hall

"No Bill whether he lives or dies is God's business and this is neither the time nor place"

"You're right" I thought for a second or two

"Give me thirty shillings of that money"

They were slid across the table to me.

I gouged a rough cross on each piece with my dirk.

We removed all his money from his pockets which thankfully still contained the five shillings he had received from Andrew. I stuffed the thirty shillings into his pocket.

"There you are Judas there's your thirty pieces of silver. You have until the cock crows in the morning after which you will be fair game to all the border families. If you try to use this money anywhere in this region it will give you away. I suggest you ride now others may not be as lenient as us"

The reverent smiled.

"You have not forgotten the bible"

"No" I replied

"But I could have used an eye for an eye"

Dodds was about to rush away when Percy returned. Grabbing his arm Percy turned him round to face the window.

"You see that nice red glow. That's your cottage burning so you need not waste your time collecting any possessions"

At this Walter bolted for the door, leapt onto his horse and galloped off never to be seen again.

Cubby then realised I had planned this.

"So that's why Percy sneaked out to burn down the cottage"

Percy, George and I all laughed.

"What's the profit in that, I asked for hay to be piled up behind the cottage and that set alight"

"Bill you're a devious bugger but I should have realised that long ago"

"Good riddance"

George shouted as he lifted his tankard.

"We knew Dodds got his money from illicit cross border trading but did not realise he was a traitor to both sides of the border"

Percy then commented.

"I had a look around the cottage; Dodds has some good gear worth a fair amount. We will get a decent price for it and you should get more than the thirty shillings back. So tonight will be on Walter Dodds"

We all raised our tankards.

"Let's drink to that"

"What about the cottage?" Percy asked

"It belongs to Dodds, but I doubt he will ever come back to claim it"

I then thought about the old woman, Bob's mother, who was still homeless and destitute. We could not sell the property so we might as well yet someone have the benefit of it. Anyway I knew she had lost her son through Dodds treachery but dare not make this public.

"Let the old woman have it she can't live the rest of her life in that wood shed"

"Why not" George agreed

"I am sure the Reverend will be happy about that"

The Reverend Hall smiled. "The Lord works in mysterious ways"

Chapter Ten

A Night Out

eeks had passed since we had exposed Walter Dodds. Nothing had been heard about him and he had ceased to be included in our conversations over supper. One night we were quieter and less jovial for no particular reason. Andrew had picked this up.

"Boys have a night out at Morebattle it's about time you had some fun. Cubby leave the bar maids alone you're spoken for"

Cubby had another suggestion.

"I have heard a new alehouse has opened in Crailing and he is selling his ale cheap to drum up business; maybe we should give it a try?"

"Why not, it's not much further away"

I should have been aware as when Cubby had a good idea it did not always work out as expected.

That night we arrived at the inn. It was busy as there had been a horse sale at Yetholm and people were calling in on their way home. We sat on a bench next to the window swilling ale. I noticed four rather scruffy men sitting in the corner.

"Who are those?" I asked Cubby

"Don't know but they look like gypsies, wherever you get horse sales you always get gypsies"

I thought he was probably right and paid them no attention.

The door then opened and in walked Andrew and John Ferniehirst. They nodded at us in recognition but sat at the other side of the room as if obeying the Morebattle landlord's instructions.

John still had a sling over his arm as it would be a while before his collar bone healed. We left them to their drinking.

They must have been to the horse sale Cubby remarked.

We noticed John was drinking very heavily and was soon quite drunk. I went outside to empty my bladder and stood alongside Andrew.

"John drinks heavily at the moment I think his shoulder is still very painful"

He felt he had to make some excuse for his brother and I respected him for his loyalty.

I just nodded and returned to my drinking.

We watched John struggle to his feet and attempt to get more ale. He dropped his purse on the floor and a large number of gold coins fell out. He tried to discreetly pick them up.

"Must be from the sale of some horses" Cubby commented.

"Yes but it has not gone unnoticed by that four in the corner"

I thought the idiot, Andrew has no chance if they get waylaid, a one armed drunk won't be much help.

"What should I do Cubby?"

"Nothing it is not our problem"

"I know but they are Mary's brothers"

"Here we go again that woman will be the death of you"

"Look I will follow them at a distance probably nothing will happen"

"Alright if you promise not to be a hero because even you can't manage to fight four people at once"

"I promise, but I won't get home until after day break Ferniehirst Castle is a good distance away"

We restricted our drinking for the remainder of the night waiting for the Ferniehirsts to leave. Eventually Andrew dragged John out helped him onto his horse and off they went.

We waited for a moment and watched the gypsies leave. Through the window could see that they headed in a different direction so it looked like my suspicions were ill founded.

"I will follow them just in case; you had better go home otherwise Helen will be worried"

Cubby compromised

"They have taken the Oxnan road; I will come with you and turn off about a mile this side of Oxnan where a track leads east for about three miles to our farm"

I agreed as I thought if anything was to happen it would before we parted company'

We soon caught up with the two brothers who were travelling slowly as Andrew had to lead his brother's horse. We kept about one hundred yards behind them hoping not to be noticed. After three or four miles we reached the track Cubby was to take home.

"I think you will be alright see you in the morning"

Cubby waved and we parted company.

About half a mile further on another track joined ours from the west. At this junction I spotted four horsemen ahead. Andrew had also seen them and stopped. He was in a dilemma he could not abandon his brother yet to stop and fight was hopeless. I had to admire him as he drew his sword and waited for the inevitable.

It was obvious the gypsies had swung around and out flanked them. They had not noticed me. I remembered Cubby's warning but the odds were only two to one so it was worth a chance. I drew my sword and charged forward. I reached the brothers the same time as the gypsies and crashed into two of them our horses falling to the ground. I killed one with my first blow but the other slashed me across the leg before I could get at him. I dispatched him quickly as well. Andrew was still on horseback fighting off the others. One decided I would be easy meat and charged at me with his horse. I side stepped and caught his right hand but not before he cut a long gash across my back. It was now two against two and they could see the tide had turned and galloped off. Andrew dismounted.

"Are you badly hurt Bill?"

"I'll be alright so long as I can stop the bleeding"

He helped me tighten my belt around my leg which was bleeding profusely thankfully the wound on my back was not too deep.

"What shall I do?" Andrew was in a quandary.

"Get John home and send someone to help me my stupid horse has ran away"

He rushed off with John still in tow.

I sat with my back resting against the hillside it was going to be a long night. When I tried to walk the blood gushed from my leg. If I attempted to walk home, I would bleed to death quickly or I could just stay still and let my life ebb away slowly. I thought my luck had run out, my horse was probably on its way to Ferniehirst Castle. If I had not accepted the gift and kept my old horse it would have headed for home which was much closer and Cubby would have known to come looking for me.

I was cursing fate now. I waited for hours trying not to fall asleep. Is this the end I thought, would the great warrior just slip away without even a whimper? I was not sure if there was a hereafter even though the Reverent Hall assured me there was. If he is right I looked forward to meeting my father, Ethel and James. I was just about to resign myself to my fate when I heard a voice that I recognised shouting my name.

"I'm here" I repeated several times.

Then this figure appeared above me. It was Mary. I looked up to see her face with the full moon behind. She looked like the statues you see in the Catholic churches; she had been aptly named.

"Where are the rest of you?"

"There is only me, the others preferred to wait until daylight"

"Yet they let you come alone?"

"They don't know I sneaked out"

She knelt beside me.

"You're in quite a mess aren't you?"

"This belt is no good it's not wide enough"

She then proceeded to remove her trousers.

"It's alright I am wearing under garments"

She ripped off one leg and bound my wound tightly. Then she split the other leg along its length to make a long bandage for my back

"I managed to catch your horse are you able to ride"

"Yes if you help me up"

She was only small but very strong.

"I'll take you home with me; we will send someone to tell Cubby where you are and what state you are in".

"Thank you for helping me"

She smiled "You would do the same for me"

"Yes but I may have an ulterior motive"

"So might I" She laughed.

She looked directly into my eyes.

"Bill, just say it"

"Say what?" I was frightened to reply

"Oh you stupid man I love you as well but you're supposed to say it first"

"I was afraid you would reject me"

"See I was right you're not afraid of risking your life against impossible odds but in some things you are a big softy"

As we rode her voice soothed the pain of my wounds. I was comfortable and could easily fall asleep but she deliberately kept me awake.

I could not remember arriving at Ferniehirst Castle that night but when I awoke I found Mary lying fully clothed on the bed next to me.

"Is it morning yet?" I uttered.

"Oh you're awake I was getting worried, yes it is morning but you have been here for two days"

"Two days?" I could not believe it.

"Yes you must have lost a lot of blood you passed out just as we got here. All I could do was to make sure you were neither too hot or too cold"

"Where am I?"

"You're in a building attached to the castle we use to lodge visitors. My father is keen to meet you but I will make sure you have a good breakfast and are clean and tidy first"

"You really are kind to me Mary"

"You know why or have you forgotten that?"

"So it wasn't just a dream?"

"No" She leant over kissed me and left to make the arrangements.

She returned with some clothes and brought a servant carrying a large bowl of warm water. She then helped me clean myself up and make myself presentable with the new clothes.

"There you are you don't look too bad if I had left you the way you were father would have thought I had brought a tramp home"

She grabbed me by the hand.

"Come on let's get this over with"

She led me across a courtyard and into the castle. As we climbed the spiral staircase I noticed it had been built spiralling in the opposite direction to usual ones. I was later told this was to favour left handed defenders as most the Kerrs were.

"Watch out for the next step it is much smaller than the others and is meant to trip attackers rushing upstairs"

"It's alright I have met them before" I replied with confidence

But I still nearly tripped and I had been warned.

We entered a large room where at the head of a table sat Sir Thomas Kerr of Ferniehirst. He was obviously well to do judging by the quality of his dress.

"You had better sit down my boy you still don't look too well"

He seemed genuinely concerned.

"Thank you" I was happy to accept his offer.

"No, thank you Bill you have done me a great service"

He moved closer to me.

"I have known about you since you killed Jock Campbell on behalf of the Cessfords and that your real name is William Charlton"

He paused.

"I never realised that I as a Ferniehirst could ever be so indebted to you"

He looked at Mary and shook his head.

"But you have created a problem for me; Mary says she is to marry you. I know you have not asked my permission as yet, I am not sure you have even asked her, but if Mary has decided I don't think either of us will have much to say in the matter. If Mary had been my son, I know my family's future would be not only secure but probably stronger. Andrew will succeed me and I am happy enough about that but Mary would have been something else"

I interrupted.

"You should be proud of Andrew he was prepared to take on four men single handed to protect his brother"

"I am; I most certainly am"

I could sense the pride in his response. Mary sat beside her father and looked at him with apprehension.

"Don't worry Mary we will sort something out. Bill as you are English you know you need to have permission of the Wardens of the Middle Marches of both England and Scotland.

We have no problem with Walter Kerr as he married a Ferniehirst but you have no chance with Sir John Forster if he knew who you really were. This will be a high profile wedding and news of it will eventually spread"

Mary was concerned.

"What can we do then?"

"The way I see it, it's in Bill's hands. I will only give my consent if he agrees that neither of you will enter England again. This is important as either of you could be tried for Treason according to border law which carries a death penalty."

"But Bill has family and property in England"

Mary realised the consequences immediately.

"Yes I know"

Thomas continued

"That is why I say it is in Bill's hands"

I had to stop Mary's concern.

"Well if that is the price I am prepared to pay it, and what family I have can always visit us"

Thomas shook my hand.

"I have not known you long Bill but that is the reply I expected"

Mary could not contain herself and hugged me vigorously.

I shouted out as she had pressed on the wound to my back.

"You're still a big softy" She laughed.

"Mary you had better get him to rest or your marriage could be over before it begins"

She took me back to my room and got me to lie down.

"I have to let Cubby know what has happened so I will send someone to tell him that you are up to receiving visitors. You certainly have a lot to tell him"

She ran off to instruct a messenger. I lay back on the bed still feeling dizzy but I could not tell you if it was through lack of blood or because of what had just transpired.

She was not away very long and returned to sit on the edge of the bed. She smiled at me.

"I am ever so happy" She held my hand.

"Will this be a handfastening?" I was not sure.

"No, father will not agree to that. He was brought up a Catholic, and will insist upon a church wedding. In these difficult times it will have to be a Protestant service but a least it will be in a church"

"When will it be then?"

"There are the bans to organise and father will want to prepare a feast so he can show off to everyone so I guess in about a month"

"That long?" I was never a very patient man.

"Look at the state of you, your leg is strapped up and you can't even lie down properly because of your back. You would not be much use to me on the wedding night at the moment would you?"

We both roared with laughter she was absolutely right.

It was then that reality hit me.

"Mary I have nothing, we cannot go to my farm in England and I am sure you would not want to share the small room I have. I know Helen would love your company but it is not like having a place of our own"

She stood up.

"Bill let's just think of one thing at a time, anyway aren't you a great believer in fate and if this is fate we must let it take its course"

Cubby arrived next morning. He, Mary and I sat at a table in what was now my room. Food for our breakfast had been supplied by one of the servants. Judging by her size I knew it would be good as it had obviously been well tested.

"So you are to be married, have you set a date yet and organised a church"

"I have done nothing yet Mary and her father seem to have taken control of the whole affair" Mary looked at me.

"Mind you, I don't mind at all I haven't got a clue when it comes to organising weddings the only decision I have to make is who will be best man, have you any suggestions Cubby?"

He looked me in disgust.

"Just joking, but you will have to behave yourself for a change"

Cubby smiled.

"I suppose I can for just one day, but you will have to do the same for me when Helen and I get round to it"

I then realised that my marriage would push Cubby into formalising his handfastening with Helen.

"We have come a long way haven't we Bill; I know we are from different sides of the border so I hope it does not become a barrier between us"

I sensed Cubby's concern.

"It can't Cubby, Mary's father will only agree to the wedding if we never go to England so I will not be able to live in my farm in Coquetdale"

This cheered him up.

"We can build you a house on my farm"

"Thanks for the offer Cubby; it may come to that but let us give fate a chance first"

I had not discussed this with Mary who was far too involved with the wedding to worry about trivial matters like where we would live.

"You're going to have to come home with me Bill, Andrew has virtually adopted you as his son and would be greatly offended if he was excluded from the wedding preparations"

Of course Cubby was right and in my excitement I had never considered Andrew. I had the greatest respect for this man even affection and would hate to upset him which was rather ironic as he was the man I was sworn to kill.

"You're right Cubby" I looked at Mary

"He would you know and anyway it would be improper for me to live here before we are married"

Mary responded shaking her head.

"Do you think that bothers me?"

"No" I replied.

"But it might bother your father"

"Alright, Cubby you had better look after him he's still not very strong; I will get someone to saddle his horse"

Mary left us alone.

"You wasted no time in asking her to marry you Bill"

Cubby patted me on the back.

"Ouch! I'm still sore you know and anyway I don't recall ever asking her"

"So she asked you then?"

"I don't recall that either she just seemed to make up her mind and expected everyone, including me, to accept it"

Cubby howled with laughter.

"The great border warrior defeated at last"

"Yes, surrendered without a fight" I joined in the joke.

Mary returned and threw me a jacket.

"You will need this yours is beyond repair"

We kissed and I hobbled away trying to keep up with Cubby.

As we rode home I told Cubby as much as I could remember about the night of my encounter with the gypsies.

He was surprised at Mary's actions.

"You mean she came to your rescue in the dead of night all on her own, that's the sort of thing you would do, so the damsel saved the white knight eh!"

I could tell he liked Mary.

"Bill I cannot wait to tell Andrew he thinks you just got wounded but it is much more serious than that"

We joked with each other all the way back to the farm.

Chapter Eleven
The Wedding

—

t was early evening by the time we reached the farm. Helen was collecting the washing from the line and greeted us.

"Just in time Cubby you can carry some of these for me" She then noticed my limp.

"How is the wounded soldier?" She said with a smile.

"His wounds are much deeper than you can see" Cubby laughed.

"Go on tell her"

"I am going to marry Mary" She could see I was excited.

"That's great, she is a lovely girl and it will be nice to have a sister in law as I never had a sister" She was thrilled as well.

I could not work out whether she had assumed the sister in law title because I was the "adopted" brother of her husband or the "adopted" son of her father. Either way I was happy for her and did not question it.

"I had better put the supper on, father is due back before long, and I can't wait to see his reaction to the news"

Andrew was later than expected so we were all sitting around the table ready for supper but would not start before the head of the house as this would be deemed disrespectful.

The door swung open and in entered Andrew kicking off his boots before sitting down with a sigh.

"What a day I have had"

"It's a good job you're sitting down we have surprising news for you"

Helen was bursting to tell him.

"Later" Andrew held up his hand to quieten her.

"How are you son" He put his hand on my shoulder showing concern.

"Not too bad" I replied

"My wounds will heal without any long term effects"

"That's good, now Helen what's this earth shattering news"

"Bill is going to marry Mary Ferniehirst" She spurted out.

"Good God!"

Andrew was stunned but managed to regain his composure.

"That's sudden, we all knew you fancied her but didn't think it was mutual"

"Neither did I" I replied

"And I could not pluck up the courage to ask her for fear of rejection but in the end it wasn't necessary as she made the decision herself"

Cubby interrupted.

"That's another example of fate that Bill is always talking about. Fate may have got him a wife but he is still waiting for it to provide a roof over their heads"

"Well Bill will always have a home here until fate gets round to providing one"

Andrew went quiet for a moment.

"Bill I'm pleased you believe in fate, I once cursed both God and fate for taking my wife and three sons from me, but never thanked them for leaving me Helen. With her and you boys I have a family again and with your news I can look forward to the future rather than brooding on the past"

Helen held her apron out and twirled around.

"Yes we have plans to make and I will need a new dress, we Cessfords can't look like the poor relations especially amongst Ferniehirsts"

Andrew smiled. "Typical woman the first thing she thinks of is a new dress, but she is right we will all have to buy new clothes, this will be a high class event involving a major border family"

"I hope things don't get out of hand. A quiet wedding suites me"

"Bill you're so naive do you not realise how famous you are and how important a family you are marrying into" He shook his head.

"Other than royalty weddings in these parts they do not come much bigger than this"

"Yes" Helen joined in still twirling around.

"All the important people will be there so I must look my best"

"For goodness sake Helen get on with the supper you're making me dizzy" Andrew turned to me.

"Do you know where and when it will be?"

"Not yet Mary says she will call in a couple of days with more details but it won't be for at least a month"

"Well at least that gives us a reasonable amount of time to prepare. Thankfully the Ferniehirsts have to do most of the arranging as it is their daughter. We only have to decide who to invite and make sure we are all presentable on the day. I will of course offer to contribute to the feast"

Andrew continued.

"Their pride will probably not allow them to accept my offer but I will make it never the less. That's enough talk about weddings tonight but you can think about who you would like to invite and maybe we can draw up a list tomorrow"

I agreed then asked what sort of day he had had as judging by his sigh it must not have been a good one.

"It's that bloody bull of mine it's as big and horny as its father Samson but not as placid. He must have got the scent of cows in the next farm and burst through the gate to get at them. No way could I coax him home till he had finished. That's why I am late. The stupid bugger has cost me a lot of money as I would have charged for his services. But at least your news has cheered me up"

We retired for the night but I must admit I did not sleep much either because the wound on my back niggled or I could not help thinking about Mary.

Next morning after breakfast I sat with Helen to prepare a list of people I would like to invite.

"You can forget about any Cessford Kerrs, Father will get the message to them which includes Cubby's Uncle Matthew's family so you only need worry about your family"

Helen was right but I hardly needed a list for my family which was only my Aunt Esther and her daughter Ella.

"But I only have two" was my reply

"I know but you have friends in Coquetdale some of whom are distant relatives. You will have to invite some of them otherwise we will only have both sides of the Kerr family"

"That's right Helen I can invite the Robson brothers and Nebby with of course their wives and even Reverend Hall. It's a pity he can't marry us but Mary's family will no doubt be organising their own priest"

"Well Bill that hasn't taken us very long. As soon as we know more details I will sent one of the farm hands to pass on the invitation"

That was it finalised in no time at all. It was probably just as well there was only a small number they would go unnoticed by Forster who had not even been asked to give permission. It's doubtful he could take any action against them but it could make life difficult if you upset the Lord Warden.

It was two days later before I saw Mary again. She arrived at mid-day when I was sitting outside the house in the sun sheltered from the wind. She sat down next to me, leaned over and kissed me.

"Missed me have you?"

I hadn't really as I knew she would have a lot to arrange and was surprised she had come so soon. This was probably not the answer she would want.

"Of course I have"

"Well Bill father has arranged the church for five weeks on Wednesday. He is very superstitious and thinks it's unlucky to have it in the latter part of any week. I didn't care what day it is so I let him have his way. Anyway it will give you plenty of time for your wound to heal"

"That's alright with me but which church and what time"

"It will be in the Jedburgh Abbey church about an hour after mid-day to give people time to get there. It is a beautiful setting close to the river and although the main abbey is in ruins it's still very impressive"

I was pleased to hear this as it was confirmation that the wedding would take place.

"Come on Bill" She grabbed my hand pulling me up and almost dragged me into the house.

Helen and Mary hugged.

"I've come to ask you something" Mary looked at Helen.

"My two sisters want to be bridesmaids so I need someone to keep them in line. Will you be a bridesmaid as well?"

"Of course" Helen held her apron and span around again.

"Father will have to get me a special dress now"

"Eh!" Mary stuttered

"I hope he will not be offended but my father insists all four of us must dress the same and has made arrangements for us all to go to Jedburgh. At his expense of course"

Helen was quick to respond.

"I think my father will be happy enough so long as your family allow him to contribute to the feast, it's a matter of pride and he has already stated he will offer to do so"

Mary laughed.

"With your father's pride and mines superstition we will have to make sure both are satisfied"

"Why does he insist we dress the same?" Helen was puzzled.

"Father says evil spirits lurk at weddings and if we all dress the same it confuses them. Cubby and Bill will have to dress the same as well"

"That's not a problem as Bill and Cubby both need some decent clothes and I will try to get father to do the same. So it looks like we will all be making a trip to Jedburgh"

I interrupted them as if offended.

"I'm pleased you girls have sorted everything out"

"Sorry Bill if it seems as if we have not consulted you"

She then laughed and hit me hard on the shoulder.

"But we have no intention of asking your opinion until we have arranged everything"

I just shook my head. I was happy enough not to be involved as I was sure I would inadvertently offend someone.

It was then that both Andrew and Cubby entered.

Andrew spotted Mary and immediately went to her kissing her on the cheek.

"This boy has been moping around for weeks like a lost puppy. Maybe now he can concentrate on his work"

Realising that it would now be dark before Mary could get home I asked.

"Cubby do you think you could see Mary safely home?"

Andrew interrupted.

"No need. I will go with her as I need to discuss details with her father. I will have a bite to eat first while Cubby saddles up my horse"

Within an hour they departed leaving Helen, Cubby and I to have supper together.

We sat and chatted until the early hours about what I can't remember but I went to bed happy and slept like a baby.

Andrew returned next morning and had come to an arrangement with Mary's father who had agreed to let him donate a cow and a couple of sheep for the feast and allow him to pay any expenses involving his side of the family. This has satisfied his pride. As Thomas was arranging the church and feast I was at a loss to see what other expenses Andrew would have other than new clothes for us. The agreement was therefore diplomatic and I could see Mary's hand in it.

Helen sent one of the farm hands into Coquetdale with invitations for my family and friends. He said they were all astonished but happy for me and that they all looked forward to the occasion.

The next few days passed slowly as I could only sit around the house generally just watching Helen work. My wounds were healing well but any strenuous work would open them up again. Helen watched over me like a gaoler no way was she going to allow me to prevent the wearing of a new dress.

It was another three days before I saw Mary again this time escorted by a couple of her father's men. I was pleased they had stopped her travelling alone.

She bounded into the house clearly very excited.

"You will never guess who is coming to the wedding"

"All right then I'll not guess so spit it out you are bursting to tell me" I was intrigued.

"James Stewart, and not only that he insists his friend John Knox conducts the service"

"Good God!" I was astounded not only would the head of the Scottish parliament be in attendance but the head of the now Protestant Church would carry out the ceremony.

So much for a quiet wedding I thought.

"How on earth has this happened?"

"News of the wedding was spread quickly and eventually reached his ears. He still thinks he is in debt to Andrew for saving his life and has not forgotten your part in stopping Forster's raid so he has insisted on going. Father is delighted as it is a boost to his status"

She then turned to Helen.

"When I return home you have to come with me as tomorrow we're all going to Jedburgh to be measured for our dresses. You men will have to make your own arrangements it's unlucky to come with us. Oh Helen they will be beautiful as Father will now spare no expense"

I was happy for Helen.

"That's fine we boys will go next week I should be healed enough by then travel without discomfort"

I was pleased for Mary and her family as this was an important event for them, but I was now worried about my friends from Coquetdale who would be attending an illegal marriage so far as the English Warden was concerned. I hoped it would not get them into trouble.

"Come on Mary let's take a walk I'm fed up with just sitting around and need some fresh air"

She took hold of my arm and helped me out of the chair. We strolled along the river bank but always in sight of the house to let everyone see we were behaving properly.

"I wish we had just run away and got married"

Mary looked me seriously then smiled.

"Run, you can hardly walk and anyway you have given up your English family to marry me I can hardly give up mine as well"

She was of course right and the way things had developed there was no way of turning back now without upsetting everyone we hold dear.

We returned to the house to find Helen all ready to go.

"You will have to tell Father I'm away; there's plenty of bread and meat I am sure you won't starve. I'm ready Mary and would rather leave so we can travel all the way in day light; I hate riding in the dark"

Mary was in full agreement.

"I don't like the dark either"

"But you went alone in the dark to rescue Bill knowing there were dangerous men about"

Helen waited for a response.

"Yes I did, but I was still anxious, only it was something I just had to do. I don't think Bill would have lived if I had waited till morning."

She looked at me and smiled.

"Time will tell if it was worthwhile"

We kissed and off they went linking arms.

The following week Cubby, Andrew and I did go to Jedburgh for our clothes. We all agreed to the same colour and style but with individual variations so we were not exactly the same. It was enough to satisfy the superstitious.

Time was now passing slowly and with now only a week and a half to go I was impatient. I was feeling much better and needed to become more active again. It was that night when Andrew came back to the house earlier than normal.

"I have just received a message from Walter they have information that there is an intended raid on his cattle. Cubby and I need to go and assist. Bill, you are in no condition to help and I dare not put you in danger so close to the wedding"

He then looked at Helen.

"Don't worry I will make sure Cubby is safe. We need to go straight away so you only need supper for you and Bill"

At this they collected their jackets and steel bonnets and departed.

Helen and I were left alone for two nights which although expected still caused us concern. It was mid-morning when I saw Andrew returning but there were no signs of Cubby.

Helen ran out of the house straight to her father.

"What's happened, where is Cubby?"

"It's alright I have left him behind to carry out some duties for Walter. We stopped the raid without anyone getting hurt so he will only be a couple of days.

I was just as relieved as Helen.

Sure enough two days later he returned with some documents for Andrew.

"Walter says you need to keep these safe as they will be difficult to replace. They are what you expected"

Andrew seemed happy.

"Come on boys it's a nice day and I don't feel like working today let's do a bit of fishing. You seem to have mended well Bill so you have no excuse not to join us"

He was right with less than a week to go to the wedding I was almost completely healed. So we grabbed our rods and headed for the river and sat on the bank side with our lines dangling in the water.

It was sunny and warm so we laid back chatting to each other not bothering too much about the fishing. It was a day I would always remember. I had a father, brother and sister and although none of them were blood relatives I don't think anyone could have a better family. I was now about to have a beautiful wife so I just lay back smiling.

"What are you so happy about?" Cubby had noticed.

I could just reply "Everything"

The next few days passed more quickly as I was now able to carry out some chores around the farm. I was still forbidden to do anything strenuous and Helen still looked over me like a mother hen.

Mary and an escort came to visit the day before the wedding just to make sure everything was in hand. She told me her father had given us the guest quarters until we had something more permanent. It was where I had been housed while my wounds had been treated. Her two sisters had been given the task of ensuring everything was clean and tidy for our wedding night.

"Is that all right" She asked

"Yes that's fine with me at least we will not have to travel far after the wedding feast. Although I don't know where we will live afterwards"

"Neither do I, but maybe this will help us find somewhere"

She handed me a leather bag. It was heavy and easy to guess the contents. It was full of gold coins.

"What's this?" I was dumbfounded.

"Father says he has been saving it for my wedding. He always thought it unfair that the boys will inherit the land so this will allow us to buy our own place. It has been his secret as he did not want anyone to marry me for my money"

"As if you would let that happen"

"Exactly" She laughed.

"But it is better to be safe than sorry"

"It's still a lot of money" I was surprised at the amount.

"Father says it is mostly from 'business' and business has been good this year"

I knew what business she meant so did not pursue the matter further.

"I will take the money home with me it will be safer in the castle until we need it. Helen will have to come as well so we girls can all leave from the castle tomorrow"

I agreed and off they went with the four riders who had accompanied Mary.

I watched her ride into the distance knowing the next time I would see her she would be walking down the aisle towards me. I could not wait for that moment.

The morning arrived soon enough. Andrew, Cubby and I got dressed in our new clothes but wore large cloaks to protect us during the journey. They were not needed as it was a glorious day.

We were early so had plenty of time to tether the horses and mingle with those who were already there. I spotted Captain Murray and his Lieutenant.

"Lost him already have you"

"Hello Bill you have got a grand day"

He shook me firmly by the hand.

"He's inside talking to John Knox and an English Priest so I doubt he's in much danger. He has a lot of Catholic enemies further north so we have to be more diligent there"

Murray gestured with an open palm.

"You had better go inside and introduce yourselves"

"Yes I think we had better there will be plenty of time to chat later"

In we entered. James Stewart spotted us and walked towards us as we approached.

"Come Andrew and I will introduce you to my friend John Knox"

He guided us forward.

"John this is Andrew Kerr the man who saved my life"

They shook hands.

"And this is Bill with his best man Cubby. I nearly introduced you as Andrew's sons but we are in church and that would have been not quite true"

Andrew responded immediately.

"But it would have been near enough so as not to offend the almighty"

James continued.

"And this is the Reverent Hall a friend of Bills I believe"

"He certainly is and he has known me longer than anyone else"

I shook his hand firmly.

"Can we have a quick word Bill?"

"Of course you can, please excuse us for a moment"

We moved to the side of the church.

"Your wedding is no longer a secret. In the past couple of days, it has been the main topic of conversation in the local inn. I think you need to warn your family and friends in Coquetdale"

"I will. I am pleased it did not put you off coming"

"I'm pleased as well John Knox has asked me to assist by reading a passage during the ceremony. It's a great honour"

"No Reverent the honour is mine"

"You and Cubby had better take a seat at the front people are starting to enter"

We both sat down. I sat slightly turned so as to see who was there.

I noticed Esther and Ella sitting with the two Robson brothers and their wives to their right with Nebby and his wife at the other side.

Matthew Kerr and his family and numerous other "Cessfords" were all sitting on the groom's side as was only to be expected. This almost balanced my side with the Ferniehirst.

I was surprised to see John Armstrong, his wife and Wanless sitting at the back. I guess as the head of a major family Mary's father was obliged to invite them.

The church was now just about full. Cubby was getting impatient.

"I'll go and see if they are here yet"

He marched quickly to the door only to swing swiftly on his heal and return.

"They're here so it will not be long now. Too late to change your mind now Bill"

"Can't do that I haven't got Mary's permission"

At this John Knox gestured us all to stand.

Mary entered with her Father on her arm followed by the three bridesmaids all of whom were dressed in white. Mary's bodice was much more elaborate being embroidered with gold thread and pearls. She had her face covered with a long veil hiding her from any evil spirits.

She had only taken two or three steps when she through back her veil as if to say I'm here evil spirits do your worst. Her father was startled but still managed a smile. He knew her well it was her day and no veil or evil spirit would hamper her enjoyment.

She walked regally towards me smiling all the way. Stopped and looked me directly in the eyes.

John Knox started with.

"Dearly beloved, we have come together in the presence of God to witness and bless the joining together of this man and woman in Holy Matrimony"

We continued to look at each other with the words of the ceremony just passing over us until we heard our names.

"Into this union Mary Kerr and William Charlton also known by some as William Kerr now come to be joined. If any of you can show just cause why they may not be lawfully wed, speak now, or else forever hold your peace"

At this point he paused.

I had visions of some representative of Forster stopping the service due to it not being authorised by the English Warden. There was silence. I should not have worried I doubt there was anyone brave or stupid enough to intervene.

The rest of the ceremony continued in its predetermined format right up to the words.

"I now pronounce man and wife"

At this point Mary put her arms around my neck and I kissed my wife for the first time. I had loved her since that meeting when she had asked. "Who is this idiot?"

Her first words to her husband were.

"I think everyone is in need of some food and drink so we had better get a move on"

Arm in arm we walked towards the door nodding to the guests. As we stepped outside Captain Murray's troupe formed an arch with their lances.

"I'm thirsty Bill let us get a drink together"

We walked to a horse trough located near the entrance to the church yard. It was fed by a spring so was good clean drinking water. A tin mug was held there by a chain obviously for the use of the congregation. Mary picked up the mug.

"Bill we must hold this together, fill it and drink. Come on this is important."

I did as I was told, filling the mug was easy but drinking it together was more difficult and we spilt most of it.

She laughed.

"I know you don't know what that was about but you will thank me for the rest of your life"

A few days later she told me why. Apparently superstition has it that if the first act of a husband is to do something his wife has requested then she will be dominant for the rest of the marriage.

She had made sure we had carried out the first act together. She saw us as equals and would not take advantage knowing I probably would not be acquainted with the custom.

We left the church yard climbed into a waiting carriage to take us to Ferniehirst Castle for the feast. As we pulled away a number of the guests threw shoes at the carriage. A good luck custom which I could not fathom and still can't.

Mary held my arm and leaned on my shoulder all the way. She was happy and so far it had been a perfect wedding.

Once at the castle we stood in the great hall at the top of the stairs greeting all the guests as they arrived.

Mary's father was first.

I shook his hand vigorously. It was the first chance I had of thanking him for his generosity.

His response was.

"I have my status to think about so I could not let my daughter live in poverty could I?"

"Of course not"

I replied with both of us knowing full well he had gone way beyond what was necessary.

"Bill we can talk later I know of a farm almost exactly between here and Andrew's farm. It is not officially for sale but I know the owner is getting on, and as he has no descendants to help, I am sure he would accept a reasonable offer"

"That would be perfect, wouldn't it Bill?" Mary was excited.

"Yes it would" I agreed.

In came John Armstrong and his wife followed by his protector Wanless.

"Bill I hope you and Mary aren't offended as we have come without an invitation"

"Don't worry, I assumed Thomas had invited you and he probably assumes I have"

"Good. I wanted to give you this"

He handed me a purse containing a substantial amount of money.

"There's no need for this" I attempted to hand it back.

"No Bill, it's far less than the ransom I would have had to pay if you had not helped my son escape Forster's men"

"That right, take it otherwise we will be offended"

John's wife intervened.

Mary responded.

"Thank you very must your gesture is appreciated"

John looked around and then whispered to me.

"Is the Kings bastard here?"

"Yes he's at the back of the hall"

"Then I will keep out of his way, not too well dressed am I?"

I knew what his pointed comment meant. James Stewart's father James V on meeting Johns' father Johnnie Armstrong was so offended by the opulence of his dress, which was much fancier than his that he had him and his followers hung.

The remainder of the guests filtered in.

Cubby and Andrew were almost last.

Mary hugged and kissed Andrew.

"Thank you for everything"

"We haven't done that much but I think this might help. Go on give it to him Cubby"

Cubby handed me a document which I recognise as the one he had given Andrew after being away helping Walter.

"Here read it"

I opened it, saw the great seal and realised its importance at once.

"Look Mary its Forster's permission for the wedding. How on earth did you manage that?"

Cubby explained.

"Andrew and I caught one of Forster's men when we stopped that raid. He did not know that Bill Kerr and Bill Charlton were the same man so he signed it without much trouble as it was much cheaper than paying a ransom. He will be annoyed when he finds out who you are but it will be too late then"

Mary hugged Cubby.

"You don't know how important this is to me; you have removed the only thing I regretted about the wedding. This will be a perfect day now, won't it Bill?"

The guests now all seated we moved to the head table. Mary and I sat in the middle with Helen and Mary's sisters to the side of Mary and her father at the end. To my side were Cubby and Andrew.

We had been seated according to tradition but not to Mary's satisfaction.

"This is all lop sided, Andrew move along one and let Helen sit between you and her husband"

It was a good move Andrew was proud to sit next to his daughter who looked beautiful in her new dress and she was happy sitting next to Cubby.

The feast was fabulous with beef, pork and lamb in abundance.

It was all washed down with ale or wine according to preference.

After the formalities of the various toasts all of which including mine were thankfully brief we were able to mingle.

We were eventually able to slip away virtually unnoticed to our room. It was a surprise Mary's sisters had sprinkled flower petals on the floor and the foot of the bed. White lace had been hung on the windows like curtains to give us our privacy but they looked nice as well.

We sat on the side of the bed wondering how to make the first move. I did not wait long. Mary stood up and removed her bodice.

"You've seen these before haven't you Bill?"

"Yes, and I got a slap for my trouble"

She sat down next to me.

"You're allowed to do more than look and I promise not to slap you"

We held each other for a while and then made love for the first time. I had the experience of a few encounters with a barmaid at Morebattle but this was intense and much more passionate altogether. It was Mary's first time but she was not the least bit nervous and confided in me later that it had never worried her in fact she had looked forward to it.

The next morning, we huddled together as the sun rose. She lay naked with her hair almost covering her face. I swept it aside allowing the back of my hand to brush over her breast. She looked at me and smiled. I had never been so happy.

"Dad, dad wake up you have been asleep for ages we need to go it'll be dark soon"

It was my son William I had fallen asleep lying with my back supported by the cairn at Windy Gyle.

"Sorry son I must have been day dreaming"

"Must have been a good dream dad you were smiling"

"Yes it was son, it most certainly was"

THE END

Historical Notes

irst and foremost, this book is meant to be just a good story and is a piece of pure fiction. However, the story is built around a framework of historical facts of the mid sixteenth century and is based mainly in the 1550's culminating in Bill's wedding which I have dated as late 1560. So as not to offend any serious historians by this mixture of fact and fiction I feel it is necessary to show the distinction between the two. In doing so I hope it stimulates interest in the history of a region in what was a turbulent time.

Times were difficult for the local population. They were constantly suffering from the continuous raids between the two countries. The quality of the land was poor and the method of inheritance did not help. Instead of land being inherited by the eldest son the custom was to split it equally between all the sons. This caused smaller and smaller farms becoming increasingly difficult for them to support their families. This created the background for reiving. The "riding" (reiving) families became active with raiding, blackmail (protection money) and ransom part of everyday life. The Wardens had the almost impossible task of keeping the law and frequently joined in or profited from these activities .

English Families

The Charlton and Robson families did live in the Tynedale and Coquetdale area but Bill his family and others mentioned did not exist. Sir John Forster was warden at this time (1560-1586) and was notorious; again his involvement in this story was fiction

Scottish Families

On the Scottish side Sir Walter Kerr was Warden (1558-1572?) living in Cessford Castle and did have a son William who would eventually become Warden (1573-1584?). Cubby his father and mother, Uncle Matthew, Andrew and Helen Kerr are inventions on my part.

Sir Thomas Kerr lived in Ferniehirst Castle and would be Warden after William Kerr (1584) but for only about a year after which the position returned to William. He did have a son Andrew and a daughter Mary but the events involving the family are pure invention.

The Elliots and Armstrongs were families allied to each other but all characters are fictional with the exception of Johnnie Armstrong who did meet an untimely death at the hands of James V. Hollows Tower or now known as Gilnockie Tower was the seat of the Armstrong family.

Sir James Stewart

Sir James Stewart did exist and most of the facts about him are true although he obviously never met Bill. He was the illegitimate son of James V and therefore half-brother of Mary (Queen of the

Scots). In 1560 he did oust Mary of Guise (Widow of James V) and with Mary the legitimate heir married to the Dauphin of France and living abroad took control of the Scottish government. He was assisted by the English crown and with his Protestant Lords of the Congregation replaced the Catholic Church. Part of his agreement with the English was to eject the French and their influence from Scotland. The Kerr family although Catholic were no friends of the French so tolerated the situation

Customs

The description of the formalities surrounding a Truce Day although brief is probably reasonably correct.

The superstition and customs of the wedding are I think appropriate to that time. Other customs such as the unblessed hand and the Charlton spur are fairly well known.

Handfastening was an informal type of marriage usually for about a year. In the remote areas of the borders they had to depend upon travelling priests. Even villages with churches did not necessarily have full time preachers. Any children born under this arrangement were legitimate even if the parents did not eventually marry.

Inns

The inns and ale houses mentioned are fictional although no doubt some existed. The inn described at Alwinton pre dated the current "Rose and Thistle" and the "Red Lion" which is now a private house. The Rose and Thistle is reputed to be where

Sir Walter Scott stayed whilst writing "Rob Roy". A nearby hall and cave are alleged to have inspired him. I take this with a pinch of salt judging by the number of "Rob Roy" caves there are. The Church at Alwinton is interesting as when extended it was stepped up into the hillside and the pathway is paved with headstones. In the early seventeenth century the vicar was ejected from the vicarage and it converted to an ale house by one of the local families so it is doubtful that an Inn existed at that time. It was not unknown for vicars to be murdered and replaced by someone nominated by a major family so the minister would have little say in the matter.

Witches

It my story the old woman was worried about being accused of being a witch. In this superstitious age this would have been a real concern. In 1590 an infamous trial took place only a few miles away at North Berwick with "witches" being executed and burnt after confessing under torture. It is said that Shakespeare who was writing Macbeth at the time was inspired to include the three witches because of this.

Gypsies

At the time this novel was set "gypsies" or as they were also known as "Egyptians" were in and out of favour with the Scottish crown. Although there is no evidence of them living at Yetholm at this time it would eventually be known as home to "the king of the Gypsies".

Hot Trod

A "hot trod" can best described as a legal posse. Within six days of an offence a hot trod can be called to pursue thieves to retrieve cattle and punish those involved. The pursuit can cross borders and can be indicated by having a burning piece of turf on the end of a lance and accompanied by riders, hounds and the sounding of horns. There is a legal obligation to assist.

Appendix

Content prompted by actual events

Some of the content of my story was prompted by actual events.

My friends Peter and Hilary De Villiers used to take me to a restaurant "The Hook Line and Sinker" in Pringles Bay, South Africa where the owner Stefan if asked what the menu was on his fish nights would reply "Fish or bugger all, what would you like?" Sadly, my friends and Stefan are no longer with us but are not forgotten.

My Uncle Jackie Moffat in WWII fought the Japanese in Burma. Back home in the UK he, my father and grandfather bred pigs so he was given the task of stealing a pig from a nearby village. He managed to acquire a youngster but its squealing alerted some Japanese on the outskirts of the village who fired at him killing the pig. Jackie also took part in the D Day landing which we have just celebrated the 80th anniversary of. I wish he had passed on more stories.

Disputes between Scotland and England were often settled by man to man combat. A usual place for these duels was Gambles Path located near the old Roman fort at Chew Green close to the border. It was here that Robert Snowdon of Hepple slew the Scottish champion John Grieves in a pitched battle with small swords. Robert was only sixteen years old at the time but would meet an untimely death when stabbed in the back trying to retrieve a stolen horse. This event is quite famous but the reason behind it is unknown to me.

The Reivers Legacy

In 1603 when James VI became James I of both England and Scotland he was determined to end the border problem. He was ruthless in his campaign with many being executed and others fled to Ireland and the new world. Some of the Graham family even changed their name to Maharg (Graham reversed). They gave their name to Robson mountain in Canada and other places in Canada and America. They have spread across the globe and one even further (Neil Armstrong). Their ancestors have provided two American Presidents (Nixon and Johnson). Without Alexander Graham Bell who invented the telephone we would not have the internet. Their influence is therefore global.

APPENDIX

Main Characters

COQUETDALE FAMILIES

Main Family

John Charlton	----- Brothers -----	William Charlton
Married Esther		Married Eleanor (nee Robson)
|		|
Daughter Ella		Son William (Bill his story)
		Married Mary Kerr
		|
		Son Young William

Alwinton pub customers

Little Willie Harry	Potts the bully (Killed by Bill)
Reverend Hall	Alwinton parson
The Robson Brothers	Coquetdale family
George and Percy	Distant relatives of Bills mother
"Nebby" Harry	Relative of Robson brothers
Tom	Nebby's pal
Walter Dodds	Informer (banished from borders)

Lord Warden English Middle March

Sir John Forster	Lord Warden of English Middle March

Holy Island

Fishermen	Cuthbert
	George
	Harry
Cart Driver	John Robson

SCOTTISH FAMILIES

Lord Warden Scottish Middle March
Sir Walter Kerr of Cessford – *Married* – Isobel Kerr a Ferniehirst

Armstrong/Elliot Alliance

Thomas Elliot	Killed by James
Mark Elliot	Thomas's Brother(Killed James but avenged by Bill)
John Armstrong	Head of family and alliance
Wanless Armstrong	One less
Thomas Armstrong	John's Son

Kerrs of Cessford

James Kerr	Cubby's Father
Ethel Kerr	Cubby's Mother
Cuthbert Kerr	Cubby
Matthew Kerr	Cubby's Uncle(Farm next door)
Andrew Kerr	Cubby's distant relative (Deputy Warden)
Bill Kerr	Andrew's son (Died from wounds by Bill's father)
Helen Kerr	Andrews's Daughter

Kerrs of Ferniehirst

Sir Thomas Kerr	Head of the Ferniehirst family Often in conflict with Cessford branch
Andrew and John	Ferniehirst Brothers Sons of Sir Thomas Kerr of Ferniehirst
Mary	Their Sister, eventually Bills wife

Other Scottish characters

Jock Campbell	Scottish Champion Swordsman (killed by Bill)
Lord James Stewart	James V's illegitimate son
Captain Murray	Commander of the lancers
John Knox	Head Scottish Protestant Church

You have reached the last page of my book
But before you close it take a look
There are many pages before the last
They're all part of a story of the past
Although its fiction its partly true
Let's hope that fate is good to you

Suggested Reading

There are numerous publications relating to the Border Reivers and I have only read a few. The following are relevant to my story.

THE BORDER REIVERS (1974)   Godfrey Watson

STEEL BONNETS (1971)   George Macdonald Fraser

PREHISORIC ROCK ART
In Northumberland (2001)   Stan Beckensall

Recommended

TOMLINSON Comprehensive Guide
to NORTHUMBERLAND (1888)   W W Thomlinson

www.ingramcontent.com/pod-product-compliance
Lightning Source LLC
Chambersburg PA
CBHW032123170626
46808CB00006B/2084